THE SH

Sharon Tregenza was born and grew up in Cornwall and lived for many years in Cyprus and the United Arab Emirates. She moved back to the UK and ran holiday businesses that included a park full of run down lodges with a bat infestation and a fishing lake (until an otter ate all the fish). She is now settled in a village near Bath, where she happily creates mystery with a touch of magic.

Sharon Tregenza's debut children's novel won the Kelpies Prize, the Heart of Hawick Award and was long-listed for the Branford Boase. She has an MA in Creative Writing from the University of Wales, Trinity St David and has recently completed a second MA in Writing for Young People at Bath Spa University.

www.sharontregenza.com

@SharonTregenza

Praise for The Shiver Stone:

An unusual and original novel which hooks you in from the start. Readers will enjoy this mysterious, lyrical adventure with a dark secret at its heart.

Steve Voake

A heart-in-the-mouth adventure story, presided over by the mysterious Shiver Stone, with 'the gentle swoosh and crackle of the waves' as its soundtrack.

Sue Purkiss

Beautifully crafted, with a plot that perfectly balances family drama with mystery. The beaches of Pembrokeshire are a wonderful backdrop to adventure!

Elen Caldecott

THE
SHIVER STONE

Sharon Tregenza

Firefly

First published in 2014
by Firefly Press
25 Gabalfa Road, Llandaff North, Cardiff, CF14 2JJ
www.fireflypress.co.uk

Text copyright © Sharon Tregenza

A CIP catalogue record of this book is available from
the British Library.

ISBN 9781910080085
ebook ISBN 9781910080092

This book has been published with the support of the
Welsh Books Council.

Typeset by: Elaine Sharples
Original cover art by Lizzie Spikes www.driftwooddesigns.co.uk

Printed and bound by: Bell & Bain

For
Jean Yvette Rosewall and
William Herbert Rosewall
Mum & Dad

CHAPTER

1

Tonight, whatever it took, I was going to catch the phantom sculptor. My dad would ground me for a million years if he knew what I was doing, but I was determined.

A full moon shone down on Carreg. It silvered the sea and, high up on the cliff, it turned the giant Shiver Stone as black as jet. I glanced up at the great megalith and made a wish. The same wish I'd been making to the Shiver Stone for over a year.

As I crept across the cool, damp sand, razor clams squirted salt water up at me from below the surface.

Finding a boulder to hide behind, I made myself as comfortable as I could. I checked my iPhone – just gone 1.00 am.

The first sculptures had appeared on the beach overnight – piles of rocks balanced on top of each other in patterns. People liked them and photographed them. We thought it was just kids mucking around. Then they got more interesting: slabs of rock with holes in, rocks made to look like people or animals; one was in the shape of a castle and another morning there was an awesome tower – must have taken ages.

The tourists loved them too. Almost every morning there were different ones. Some disappeared and some changed. It was the talk of the village – no one knew who was doing it. It was a real mystery.

It had been going on for weeks and I was determined to find out who was doing it. Even if it meant sneaking out on my own after midnight. I'd see who it was. I'd get the mystery sculptor on video.

Bubbles of sound floated down from the village – shouts and laughs. Holidaymakers were enjoying the very last of a warm summer night.

Here, on the beach, everything was quiet – just the gentle swoosh and crackle of the waves.

I waited.

Minutes later I heard the crunch of footsteps on pebbles. I ducked down behind my boulder. Dragging my hood up over my head, I curled into a ball to make myself as small as possible.

My heart beat louder and, for the first time, I wondered if this was such a good idea, being here alone on the beach in the early hours. Maybe the phantom sculptor didn't want to be discovered. Maybe he was some crazy, who…

Someone poked me in the ribs. I yelped with fright.

'It's me. It's me. Sorry, I didn't mean to scare you.' Looking down on me and laughing was Linette, my dad's girlfriend.

'What are you doing here?'

'I followed you.'

I huffed. 'How did you know where I'd be?'

'I heard you telling Becca on the phone.'

'You listened in on my private conversation?'

'Yup. Here's a tip, Carys Thomas. If you don't want people to be suspicious – don't whisper.'

I gritted my teeth and glared at her.

She didn't look at all bothered. 'I knew if I told you not to go you'd ignore me. Your dad's at sea so he's not here to stop you. I thought the best thing to do was keep you company.'

'I don't want your company.'

Linette shrugged. 'Tough.' She wriggled down beside me. 'Squidge over.' Elbowing me into a crevice, she rummaged in a bag and brought out two Mars bars. 'No need to starve while we wait, eh.' She offered me one.

I wanted to say no but… 'Thanks,' I muttered. 'If you're staying you'll have to keep quiet for a change.'

'I can do quiet,' Linette said, rustling the Mars bar paper loud enough to frighten a lion.

The next hour consisted of Linette moaning about how cold she was, how uncomfortable she was and how stupid the whole idea was. I spent the time shushing her and telling her to shut up. The distant voices of late-night revellers grew fewer and fainter, and then stopped all together.

The sea whooshed onto the beach and slid back

with a whisper. I felt drowsy and rested my head on my arm against the boulder. I must have nodded off, because next time I looked, a hooded shadow, hands in pockets, was creeping along the water's edge.

Linette was snoring softly beside me. I nudged her. 'It's him,' I whispered. She woke with a start but, for once, was silent. She nodded.

My heart rate increased as the man stopped just a few metres in front of us.

Quickly, without hesitation, he began to build. He sorted large rounded pebbles, weighed them in his hands, smoothed them, and then accepted or discarded them. The stones ground and clacked as he built one on one on one.

I was so fascinated I almost forgot to video him. I slipped my iPhone from my pocket. I could hear Linette breathing heavily with excitement. She raised her eyebrows at me.

I wedged myself between two rocks with just enough space between them to get my phone in position. I pressed the video button.

Once he stepped back to take a look at what he'd created. He put his head on one side and pulled up his sleeves. He worked even faster, picking rocks it seemed at random. Before long we could see what he'd made.

It was beautiful. What began as a jumble of mismatched stones was now an almost perfect spire. About two metres high it cast a long black shadow in the moonlight. It looked – magical.

He turned in my direction, and almost as if he knew we were there, swiped back his hood. We had a clear view of the beard and the long blonde plaits of … the sculptor?

I mean, *the* sculptor. It was Tristan Penaluna, a local artist: a real sculptor. He was the one everyone thought of first when the strange stone creations began. But he'd denied it was him and so guesses grew more and more ridiculous as we tried to figure out who was building them.

I was disappointed. I mean it would have been more fun if the mystery person was Daisy at the gift shop or Dylan our postman. But, anyway, I had the evidence now and the mystery was solved.

Tristan left as silently and sneakily as he arrived.

As soon as he was out of earshot Linette blew her breath out between her lips. 'Not much of a mystery there, then. I can see the headlines now: mystery sculptor turns out to be … a sculptor.'

She groaned, stretched, and kneeded the small of her back. 'Enough of this silliness. I'm for my bed.'

Back in my bedroom I rubbed my eyes and peered out of my window across the bay and up to the Shiver Stone. Dawn lightened the sky in streaks and the first gull squawked. I knew that Dad, out fishing on his beloved *Sea Spirit*, would be able to see the Shiver Stone too.

I thought about my night's adventure. It was a bit of a let down. I was so tired I didn't bother to get out of my clothes. I kicked off my shoes, yawned, and flopped onto my duvet. But, just before drifting off to sleep, I had an idea.

'Television?' Linette said the next morning. 'I don't know about that. It's only a little bitty film you took on your phone. Orange or apple juice?'

'Neither. It's a good little bitty film though. Look at it on my laptop.'

It was good. The bright moonlight helped and you could clearly see the hooded figure building the spire. Then, at the end, Tristan looked right into the camera and there was a full shot of his face.

'Hmm, not bad,' Linette said. 'I do have a cousin who works for Radio Pembrokeshire; they might be interested. Could give her a ring I s'pose.'

Dad thought it was a good video too. Luckily for me, Linette decided to leave out the bit about me being on the beach on my own until she got there.

That's how it started. My fifteen minutes of fame. Interviewed on Radio Pembrokeshire first and then the local papers picked up the story. And then, three days later, the phone call from BBC Wales.

I rang my best friend. 'I'm going to be on telly now, Becca, pretty cool huh?'

'That's nothing,' she said. 'My uncle Bryce has been on telly loads of times cause he's on the Tenby lifeboat crew.'

I think Becca was jealous.

The telly thing was great, but Linette had to be there too, which was annoying. You'd think the whole thing was her idea – she didn't stop talking. I hardly got a word in. They did show my phone video though.

We didn't know then how it was going to change the lives of several people. Forever.

CHAPTER

2

It was all so exciting. I didn't think about Tristan's reaction. Not until someone told Dad he wasn't happy, not happy at all.

So, when Tristan Penaluna strode into the Crab's Claw shouting, 'Carrrrrrys!' I thought, *Now I'm in trouble.*

He had two buckets of candyfloss tucked under one arm and Tia, his dog, under the other.

'This is for you, Carys.' He passed me one of the buckets. 'To say thank you for the telly thing.'

'You're not mad at me?'

'No. I've got a load of commissions since you showed the world who the secret sculptor was. Not only that, something much more amazing has happened.' He lifted the other bucket of candyfloss and winked at me as if we shared a secret. 'This is for someone very special.'

He sat at the nearest table.

As I said, Tristan has a beard and wears his blond hair in plaits and sometimes, like today, he wears a red bandana around his head too. Dad likes country music and there's a singer called Willie something. Tristan looks like him, only younger.

He's quiet, a bit secretive really. Everyone knows everything about everyone in Carreg but no one knows where Tristan comes from, or what he did before he came. He's okay, but the best thing about Tristan is his dog, Tia. Tia is tiny – a Yorkie with bright black eyes and silvery fur. I wish more than anything in the world that she was mine.

Linette came out and handed him his coffee and a menu. Tia struggled to get to me and he passed her over without a word. As he did, I saw his weird tattoo again from his elbow to his wrist in thick black ink: *Vulpes Vulpes*.

I asked him once what it meant but he just rolled down his sleeve and changed the subject. Like I said, a bit of a mystery man.

I rubbed my face in Tia's furry tummy and she squeaked with pleasure.

'Carys, will you take Tia for a walk? I'll give you a pound.'

Linette saw the candyfloss and piped up in a second, 'She can't eat sticky stuff because of her brace, Tristan.'

I hate candyfloss but I heard myself say, 'You can't tell me what I can and can't eat.'

'Fine.' Linette was angry. 'Have what you want then. But don't blame me when your dad's annoyed.' She bustled off back inside the café. Tristan handed me Tia's lead.

I cuddled Tia and she licked at my face with her little pink tongue.

'Harbour?' I whispered and her tail wagged like crazy.

A crash made everyone jump.

I turned to see Tristan standing still as a statue, staring across the road. He looked terrified. His coffee cup lay shattered on the ground by his feet.

'Stop those damn seagulls knocking things off the tables,' Linette called.

'No, it's not…' I began.

With a shudder, Tristan came to life. He bolted. He raced to his motorbike, parked outside the café. I watched as, without looking back, he kicked frantically at the starter. His tyres screeched up St Winifred's Hill. At the zebra crossing people scattered in panic. A woman screamed but he didn't seem to notice, he just roared off like a madman.

Linette and I stared after him, then she bent down to sweep up the broken pieces of crockery. 'What's up with him?'

'Dunno,' I said. 'It was like he was frightened of something.'

'Look, he's forgotten his candyfloss.'

I held up the cuddly bundle in my arms. 'He's forgotten Tia, too.'

Linette took the dustpan inside. The Crab's Claw was busy and I knew, if I didn't escape soon, I'd be roped in to help. I clipped the lead to Tia's collar.

Straightening up, I bumped into someone standing right behind me.

He smiled. 'That man – the one that just left on the bike. That was Tristan Penaluna, wasn't it?'

I nodded.

'He's an old friend of mine from Uni. Haven't seen him in years. Be good to catch up.'

He stretched out his hand to stroke Tia. She gave a long, low growl and he edged backwards. He wore sunglasses with Ray-Ban written on the lens. They scooped around his face like a visor and were so dark I couldn't see his eyes. 'Know where he lives?' he said.

I trusted Tia's instincts.

'No.'

'What are you talking about, Carys? Of course you know where Tristan lives,' Linette said. I made a face at her but she ignored me. 'Halfway up St Winifred's Hill there's a lane on the right. At the end you'll find Hug Howell's place. Tristan rents a kind of shed on her land.'

The man thanked her and asked for a cappuccino.

He shook a pile of orange tic tacs into his hand and tossed them into his mouth. Now that he'd got his information he'd lost interest in me.

I watched him as he sat in the same chair

Tristan had just left. He rubbed his chin. He had one of those trendy beards that make a thin dark line from ear to ear along the jaw. No moustache. I wondered about that beard. How could he keep it the same length, unless he woke up every day and shaved off just one day's worth?

My daydreaming cost me.

'Dishwasher needs emptying, Carys,' Linette called.

'I've got to take Tia for a walk.'

'You can do that later, we're busy.'

'But she needs to pee.'

Linette frowned. I knew she didn't believe me, but she couldn't take the risk of a dog peeing right in front of her customers.

'Go on then,' she snapped.

As soon as the traffic lights turned red I gave a quick glance right and left, tucked Tia under my arm and darted across the road.

Summer in Carreg is crazy. Loads of tourists come for our beaches because they are brilliant – miles of clean golden sands. Tenby is famous too, and it's only a few miles up the coast. I don't blame people for wanting to holiday here but it's a pain. I like the winter when the sea and sand belong to just us again.

It's too noisy with all the people and traffic by the café, but down at the harbour, even in summer, it's quieter. I walked Tia past a group of yellow buoys and a giant coil of rusty chain. The sea smell is always strong here and I breathed it in – salty, fresh.

From the top of a mast a huge gull watched Tia with hunger in its eyes. I picked her up and held on tight. Gulls will eat pretty much anything and I wouldn't put it past this one to have a peck at her.

The gull flew off with a screech.

Dad was working on his boat. He waved and I waved back. He cupped his hands around his mouth and shouted, 'Thought you were helping Linette today?'

'Tristan left Tia behind. I'm taking her for a walk,' I called back.

He nodded. 'Coming aboard?'

I shook my head. 'See you later.'

I ran Tia around the harbour until she was panting with the heat. I walked back through the crowds of visitors and the smells of suntan lotion and fish and chips.

The guy with the skinny beard and sunglasses was gone. I asked Linette about him.

'Seemed keen to catch up with Tristan. Asked a lot of questions. Tristan will be happy to see his friend after all these years.'

I wasn't so sure. There was something about him I didn't like.

I found a cool spot out the back for Tia, gave her a bowl of fresh water, and settled her down in an empty Walkers' crisp box. She fell fast asleep.

The café was crowded all afternoon and I was kept busy filling and emptying the dishwasher.

Every time I got bored I sneaked off out the back and sat in the shade with Tia. It was easy to spot Linette coming. Her hair is dyed that bright cartoon red, the red that's not even pretending to be natural.

She gave up on me after a while. 'It's harder work chasing after you, Carys, than it is doing it myself.'

I fed Tia tiny bits of fresh ham and stroked her soft fur.

I didn't want this Saturday job in the Crab's Claw and Linette didn't want me there. Dad thought it would be a good idea for us to get to know each other better. It wasn't.

At five o' clock, when Linette closed the cafe for the day, Tristan still hadn't come back for his dog.

'Better phone him,' she said.

'He hasn't got a phone.'

'Not even a mobile?'

'No, he says it fries your brain.'

'Reckon his brain is already fried,' Linette said. 'Okay, take Tia up to his place but come straight home after. I'm making dinner for the three of us tonight.'

'Hmm.'

'What?'

'Does that mean Dad's off fishing then?'

'Yes. And I'm staying the night to look after you, whether you like it or not.'

'I'm twelve. I can look after myself.'

'Look, I'm tired, Carys. Just get rid of the dog, will you.'

It was cool and quiet along the lane. There was a low buzz coming from Hug Howells' beehives and, in the distance, the swoosh of the sea. I took my time enjoying every minute with Tia. I pretended she was mine.

I was daydreaming again. I was thinking how

good it would be if Tia slept on my bed every night; if she cuddled my feet when I was cold; if she licked my nose to wake me up…

A bee buzzed close to my face and I flicked it away.

That's when I got the creepy feeling. You know – when your neck tingles, when it feels like someone is watching you, that creepy feeling.

I scooped Tia into my arms and turned full circle. I couldn't see anyone but the silence wasn't peaceful anymore, it was scary.

I was past Hug's house and could see Tristan's shed set back in the trees. I started to run towards it when a loud voice shouted, 'Hey!'

I jumped so hard I almost dropped Tia.

Skinny beard man was leaning against the wall. The sun glinted off his sunglasses so they looked like huge insect eyes.

My heart beat fast.

He walked slowly towards me. 'Don't think he's here. Know where he could be?'

I shook my head. Tia started her low growl.

This time he laughed. 'Don't think the pup likes me much.'

I didn't answer. As he got closer, I backed away.

'Don't be scared. Here have a tic tac.'

'I'm not scared,' I lied.

'Damn, look at me offering sweets to a kid. You must know never to take stuff from a stranger and then here's me … sorry about that.'

'S'okay.'

Behind him was the path to Hug's house. I knew, if I needed to, I could run fast and hard and be banging on her door in seconds.

'I'm Kemble Sykes,' he said, 'and I know your name is Carys.' He stretched forward as if to shake my hand and Tia went berserk, yapping, snarling and struggling furiously to get at him.

He laughed and raised both arms in a gesture of surrender. With a shock I recognised his tattoo. From his elbow to his wrist in thick black ink I read *Vulpes Vulpes*.

CHAPTER
3

It took me a while to control Tia. I'd never seen her like that but, tiny as she was, I knew those teeth of hers were needle sharp. I daren't let her go. She wriggled and twisted and fought to be free, yapping all the time. It was so out of character I laughed.

Gradually she calmed down and, when I looked up again, skinny beard guy was gone. I peered up and down the lane. Nothing. Nothing but the gentle buzz of Hug's bees and the sea's swish in the background.

I thought about the tattoo. Two men with the same words needled into their skin. What did it mean – a secret club?

Tia squirmed so I let her down. She peed on a dandelion.

'Well, Tia, it looks like...' I tried his name out, 'Kemble Sykes was right about one thing, Tristan's not here. There's no sign of his bike.'

His motorbike was hard to miss. Not too many bikers have a pink dog carrier strapped between the handlebars.

'Better check inside, though.'

Tristan's house is a metal shed in a field beside Hug Howell's place. It's like a huge barrel cut in half and laid length ways on the ground. He's painted it with splodgy blocks of colour. I knocked on the door – a door that looked like it had been cut out with a giant tin opener.

'Tristan? Tristan? It's Carys. I've got Tia.'

I'd been to his place plenty of times, mostly to get Tia. If he's busy or sick Tristan pays me to walk her. I'd do it for nothing. Haven't told him that though. I pulled at the door and it rattled open with a horrible tinny screech where the edge caught on the gravel.

'Tristan?'

I slipped Tia's lead off and she leapt onto the sofa. She lay with her head on her paws looking up at me with a sad expression.

'I dunno where he is, girl,' I said.

From the outside it was just a broken-down old shed but inside he'd made it nice. Light shone in through three small windows cut into one side and a huge one in the roof. I didn't know what to do next. Take Tia home? Dogs aren't allowed in the flats, as Dad keeps reminding me. But I couldn't leave her here on her own. What if he didn't come back?

A bee landed on a map of Pembrokeshire on the wall beside me. I watched it crawl from coast to coast, from Fishguard to Tenby.

Tristan's shed smelled like the inside of a cave. The stone dust from his sculptures was everywhere. I sneezed.

At the far end was a proper door with a bar across it.

'Tristan?'

I'd never been in that room before. It's where he worked and he was secretive about it. I don't know what he carved or sculpted up here alone in his hot tin shed.

The whole thing, with Tristan racing off in a blind panic, with the creepy Mr Skinny Beard hanging around, was making me nervous.

My hand shook as I opened the door. It was gloomy inside, the dust thick, and I coughed. I could only make out shadows. I felt for a switch and clicked. Light lit the room like a sharp shock and I saw it – the thing in the corner.

Its huge mouth grinned, exposing razor sharp shark's teeth beneath a grotesque nose. It stood on the chair, its vicious eyes glinting at me.

With a shriek I turned and ran. My heart banged in my chest. I ran as fast as I could, out of the room, out of the shed. Tia hurtled after me barking and nipping at my ankles. We shot out of the door together and barrelled straight into someone standing right outside.

I screamed again.

Thinking about it now, it's no wonder the woman and boy looked at me like I was a lunatic. I must have frightened the hell out of them. She grabbed my arm as I tried to push past.

'What is it? What's the matter, child?'

'Troll!' I jabbered. 'Shark's teeth. Quick, run!' I struggled to get away but her grip was strong.

'Wait!' she said, 'wait right here. You too, Jago. I'll go see what this is all about.'

'No don't go in…'

'Tristan?' she shouted, 'Tristan, are you in there?' She disappeared into the shed.

There was the creepy silence again. Tia scrabbled at my legs, so I hoisted her up onto my shoulder.

I'd moved far enough away from the shed to make a run for it if I needed to, but curiosity held me there. The boy was about my age. He flicked his eyes from me to the door of the shed and back to me again. Scared as I was, I thought: Weird looking kid. Pale face, and white-blond hair flowing over his shoulders. He looked a bit … ghostly. He reminded me of someone.

The screech of the metal door made us both jump. The woman was back.

'It's not a troll, dear. It's a *coblyn*, if I'm not mistaken. Tristan hasn't lost his touch, I see.' She raised her pencilled-on eyebrows at me like people do when they expect you to know something. 'It's a statue of a *coblyn*?'

'What?' the boy and I said together and we laughed. He didn't look ghostly when he laughed. Nice teeth, I thought.

'*Coblynau* are mine spirits, they live in the coal mines,' the woman said. 'Nice enough most of the time but given to throwing stones, I believe. I did a class on Welsh mythology when I was in Uni.' She was obviously enjoying the chance to show off what she knew. 'Someone commissioned the sculpture, I suppose.'

'It's a statue? But it's wearing clothes.'

'Hmm, nice touch. Aren't you a bit too old to be frightened by goblins, dear, real or stone?' She wrinkled her painted eyebrows at me.

The boy laughed and I felt stupid. 'It was dark, I couldn't see…'

'And why don't you explain why you're sneaking around in Tristan's place, anyway?'

'Sneaking? I wasn't sneaking anywhere.' I glared at her. I'd made a complete fool of myself, but I wasn't going to be accused of sneaking by some stranger who knew nothing about me.

As if he'd read my thoughts the boy said, 'Drop it, Mum. You don't know who she is or why she's here.'

The woman's frown turned to a sheepish smile. 'You're right, Jago. I'm sorry, dear. Put it down to nerves. I'm very nervous. Where is Tristan?'

'Don't know.' I shrugged.

She turned to her son. 'Come in and see some of your father's extraordinary work, Jago.'

Father? Of course. That's who the boy looked like. He looked like Tristan.

'I'm Polly Pepper,' she said, holding out her hand. I snorted but managed not to laugh. Polly Pepper? What kind of dumb name was that? It sounded like a nursery rhyme.

I shook her hand. It was limp and cold, like a fish.

'This is my son, Jago. He hasn't seen his father since he was two. He abandoned us ten years ago. Just disappeared. Didn't bother to contact us.' She spoke quickly, with anger in her voice.

The boy stared down and kicked at the gravel. 'That's enough, Mum. She doesn't want to know our life history.'

But I did! This was all news to me.

A bee buzzed between us and a look of sheer panic came over the woman's face. 'Bee! Bee! Quickly, get inside!'

A bit over the top, I thought. But I scrambled back into the shed with them.

I didn't like being in Tristan's place when he wasn't there, it didn't feel right.

But Polly wasn't worried about it. She picked up a kettle, lifted the lid and sniffed for some reason. Then she filled it with water and lit the small gas stove. While she searched through the cupboards, Jago sat on the sofa looking as uncomfortable as I felt.

'I wouldn't have bothered but Jago should at least meet his father, don't you think?' Polly said. She didn't wait for an answer. 'We saw him on TV – you know the beach prank thing? That's how I found out where he was.'

'I did that,' I said. 'I took that video. I was on telly too.'

Polly wasn't interested. 'Nice, huh? Good father, huh? And now this… He knew we were coming. I can't believe he'd run off and leave us again.'

She sniffed and I saw she was close to tears.

I tried to say I thought Tristan might have been running from skinny beard man, but again she ignored me.

'Don't know why I thought this was a good idea,' she said.

Tia wriggled in my arms so I dropped her onto the rug. She peed. I pretended not to notice. So did Jago.

Then Tia did an odd thing – for her anyway. She ran over to the boy and threw herself onto his lap. She licked his face like crazy, doing her happy squeaks and snorts. He laughed and rubbed his nose into her fur.

'She doesn't usually go to strangers.' I felt a bit peeved. Jealous even.

'I'm very much a cat person myself.' Polly looked disapproving. 'We've got five.' She tossed back her hair and tugged at both ends of the long silky scarf around her neck. 'We've travelled from Bristol so that Jago can meet his father … and meet him we will. Even if he's hiding from us. You know him. You can help us find him.'

I sneezed. Now that the door was open the dust swirled in the draft. Then Jago sneezed and Tia leapt out of his arms in fright. Even Polly laughed this time. She seemed less angry.

'Where's this goblin then?' Jago said.

'*Coblyn*, dear, remember? It's like a Welsh version of the Cornish Knocker, little people who live in mines.'

'Whatever.' Jago flicked his hand at his mother.

God, how could I have forgotten the monster in

Tristan's workroom? I nodded towards the end of the shed.

Jago tucked Tia under his chin and peered in. His free arm held the doorframe. I think he was getting ready for a quick escape.

'Yes, take a look at your father's work,' Polly said. She was helping herself to coffee and sounding happier.

'Wow!' Jago pulled his head out of the doorway faster than he'd put it in.

I crept up behind him, steeled myself and peeped under his arm into the room. It still frightened the hell out of me. A closer look showed massive ears and the eyes looked so real, so spiteful.

'It's only small though,' Jago said.

'Yeah, but it's got real clothes on, that's what so creepy. And it's standing on a chair,' I whispered. 'Is that a miner's lamp it's carrying, and a hammer?'

'I think it's a fossil pick,' Jago said.

'Fossil pick, okaaay.' I've got a right geek here, I thought.

'Jeez, that is really ugly. No wonder you were scared. I would be if I came across that by accident in a dark room.' Then he added, 'I wouldn't have run away though.'

'Yeah, right.'

Tia sneezed so violently her whole body leapt in Jago's arms and we laughed.

Polly's sudden scream cut through our laughter. We spun around to find her standing in the middle of the shed, holding her neck and whimpering.

'I'm stung, Jago. I'm stung!' Her voice rose to a shrill cry.

'Oh my God! Mum?' Jago dropped Tia almost without noticing.

I stood still, amazed by all the fuss. Okay, a bee sting hurts but…

'The pen, Jago, it's in my bag. Get my pen!'

Now she's going to write about it? I was confused.

Jago leapt to her handbag and searched frantically inside. With a sob of panic he scattered the contents onto the sofa.

'It's here! Mum, it's here!' But as he handed her a plastic tube her body crumpled and she collapsed to the floor. There was a loud crack as her head hit the edge of the coffee table.

Polly Pepper lay sprawled on the rug. A trickle of blood ran from her painted eyebrow down into her hair. She was pale as death.

CHAPTER

4

'Muuuuuum,' Jago sobbed, dropping to the floor beside her.

It all happened so fast I couldn't think clearly. I stood rooted to the spot. Tia was obviously as confused as I was and darted backwards and forwards at Polly, yapping excitedly. She thought it was a game. I scooped up the little dog, ushered her into the workroom and closed the door.

Jago leapt up again. 'The phone. Where's the phone? We need an ambulance. She's allergic to bee stings. Badly allergic. She could die.' He was struggling to open a plastic tube he'd taken from her bag.

Polly was breathing oddly – fast and wheezy.

'I've got my mobile?'

'Dial 999!' Jago screamed.

With trembling fingers I dialled.

'Tell them it's anaphylactic shock. Tell them to get here right away.'

'Tell them it's what…?'

A voice on the phone asked me which service I needed.

'Ambulance. Quickly.' I could hear my voice trembling.

'Ambulance, what's the full address of the emergency, please?'

I told her where we were.

'Okay, tell me exactly what's happened.'

'This woman, a bee sting, it's … it's…'

'Anaphylactic shock,' Jago shouted at me. He shook his mother's shoulder. 'Mum, Mum, I've got the EpiPen. What do I do?'

I repeated what he told me to the emergency operator without taking my eyes off Polly. She was turning blue and her face and neck were swelling fast.

'The ambulance is on its way,' the calm voice said.

'Tell them she's unconscious,' Jago wept.

I was shaking so hard it was difficult to hold onto my phone. Again I repeated what he said.

'Do you know how to place someone in a recovery position?' the operator asked.

'Recovery position?' I shouted at Jago.

He shook his head, looking devastated. He was still fumbling with the pen thing, his whole body shaking uncontrollably.

'Do you have an EpiPen?' the voice said.

'Yes, her son's here, he's got the pen,' I blurted.

'Tell him to...'

'I can't do it. I can't do it,' Jago sobbed.

Without thinking I shoved my phone at him and grabbed the pen. I wrestled it free from the tube. It was like a syringe. My stomach churned.

As the emergency operator gave instructions to Jago he repeated them to me. 'There is a black tip on the small end of the EpiPen. DON'T put your fingers on this, it's where the needle comes out.'

I nodded.

I followed the directions from Jago. His voice grew stronger and his hands stopped shaking. The world seemed to fade away as we concentrated on every single word the operator said.

'…and gently but FIRMLY jab the black tip into her outer thigh.'

I did something I never expected to do in the whole of my life. I brought my fist down with a thump and forced a needle into someone's leg. Polly didn't even flinch.

Together we counted off the ten seconds that we were told to keep the needle in.

When we reached seven we heard the Whaaa Whaaa Whaaa of the ambulance siren. It pulled up outside with a screech of brakes and within seconds paramedics took over. Polly was placed on a stretcher and bundled into the ambulance where they gave her oxygen. I was thrilled to hear her groan.

One of the paramedics told us what a brilliant job we'd done. How we'd probably saved her life. It didn't really sink in. I was just so relieved that they were there to take over. Jago was bustled in beside his mother and just had time to give me a weak wave before the ambulance, siren still screaming, made its bumpy way back along the lane.

And I was alone again. The silence heavy around me. Only then did I fully realise what might have happened. That Jago's mother might have died there on the floor of Tristan's shed. My whole body shook.

A frantic yapping brought me to my senses and I freed Tia from the workroom. I felt so weak I knew I couldn't walk home. With trembling hands I called my dad's mobile, went outside and flopped down on the grass to wait.

A bee landed on a nearby foxglove. I watched it crawl inside the purple cup and disappear. It was hard to believe that something so tiny could cause so much drama.

Dad was there in minutes to pick up Tia and me.

Linette was delighted with my story. She loves her soap operas and this was more real life drama than she could wish for.

'A runaway sculptor, a mysterious wife and son, and a life-threatening situation – all in one day.' She counted them off on her fingers.

'Don't forget the guy with the skinny beard,' I added.

'Hmm, mysterious stranger too. Yummy stuff.'

Dad laughed, then looked serious. 'You were amazing, Carys.'

'Jago was too,' I said.

'Yeah, but you stuck the needle in.'

I didn't want to think about that bit. It made my stomach turn over.

We were outside on the balcony. Up on the cliff the Shiver Stone darkened against the sky as the sunny afternoon turned to evening. It was getting cooler by the minute, but there were still people on the beach. Kids and adults shouted and played on the sand and splashed in the sea. Two seagulls perched on next-door's railings and eyed our lasagne. Tia, after a bellyful of minced beef and grated cheese, slept, curled up on my lap.

'What about the boy?' Dad said.

'What about him?'

'Where will he go if his mother has to stay in hospital?'

I hadn't thought about that. 'He told the ambulance crew they were booked into the caravan site.'

'He can't sleep in a caravan on his own.'

Linette came back out with a bowl of fresh strawberries and some cream. She heard what

Dad said. 'He could stay here, if it's okay with you, Dai?'

'I'm off fishing. It would be up to you to keep an eye on him,' Dad said.

'S'okay.'

'You haven't asked whether I mind him being here,' I huffed.

'Well?' Dad said.

I hesitated. I have to admit the whole thing was pretty exciting. With my best friend Becca off staying with her dad in Swansea, things had been boring lately.

'I don't care,' I said.

'Right. Let's finish up here and get to the hospital and see what's what.' Dad shoved a huge strawberry in his mouth, stalk and all.

Someone had washed off Polly's eyebrows so her face looked bald. There was a cut with stitches over one eye where she'd hit the coffee table when she fell. Jago sat huddled up in a chair by her bed.

'She'll need to stay in another day or two at least. There's a possibility of concussion from that head wound too,' Dr Dylan told Dad and Linette.

Polly grabbed my hand with both of hers and wouldn't let go. 'Jago told me what you did. You saved my life. How can I ever thank you?'

It was really embarrassing. I tried to tug my hand away without hurting her feelings. 'S'all right.'

Dad asked her if she'd like Jago to come home with us until she got out of hospital.

She looked a little uncertain. 'Thank you. I don't know what to say.'

Dr Dylan stepped forward. 'You can say yes, Ms Pepper. Dai Thomas has been my friend since nursery school and Linette is my niece. Carys there has called me Dr Dylan from the minute she could speak, haven't you, menace?'

I grinned.

'We dump our six-year-old twins on them sometimes. They'll look after your boy until you're okay to go home,' he said.

'My dad, has he turned up yet?' Jago looked more miserable than ever.

Linette put an arm around his shoulder. 'I'm sure he'll be back as soon as he hears what's happened. But until then you can stay with us. Okay?'

He looked at his mother and she nodded. 'I'll

be fine in a day or two. No point this spoiling your holiday, Jago.'

'Bit late for that,' he mumbled.

Because of the view from the balcony, most people go, 'Oh wow!' when they come into our flat. Jago didn't say, 'Oh wow.' He didn't say anything.

Dad had to leave, to catch the tide, but Linette tried cheering him up. She can talk for Wales. But even she gave up after an hour of nothing but grunts.

He did smile once when Tia licked his nose.

I Googled '*Coblynau*' on my laptop and read: '*Coblynau* are half a yard long and hideously ugly. They wear miners' clothes and carry work tools and lamps. If one is angry it can cause rock slides.' Then I Googled 'fossil pick' and found out it was a pointed-tip rock hammer used by geologists.

'Emailing your friends?' Linette asked. She was making up the sofa bed in the lounge for Jago.

'Yeah.' I slammed the laptop closed. Now I'm being a geek checking out this stuff, I thought.

I texted my friend Becca to tell her what had happened with Polly and Jago and Tristan. She texted back saying 'cool' and then gave me a list of all the amazing stuff she was doing with her dad.

By ten o'clock I was tired. I tucked Tia under my arm and sneaked her into my room before Linette had a chance to moan about it.

I struggled awake from a nightmare of a giant bee trying to eat my face to find Tia scrabbling at my head to go out.

I opened my door and, still half asleep, trundled after her into the lounge to let her onto the balcony.

Someone was leaning over the railings. It startled me and I shrieked.

Jago turned sharply. 'Sorry! Couldn't sleep.'

'Forgot you were here,' I said, rubbing my eyes.

I joined him outside. My gaze automatically went up to the dark shadow of the Shiver Stone. In the bright silver moonlight it looked its dramatic best. A black giant of a stone keeping watch over our little village – keeping guard.

'It's getting cold,' he said.

Tia peed on the balcony and I promised myself I'd clean it up before Dad or Linette noticed.

Jago and I wandered back inside. He sat on the edge of the sofa bed. I got an apple from the fruit bowl and offered him one. He took it.

'Does that hurt?' he said.

'What?'

'The brace on your teeth.'

'No.'

We sat without speaking for a while and then he said, 'She's nice.'

'Who?'

'Your mum.'

'She's not my mum, just my dad's girlfriend, and she's not nice.'

'Oh.'

Silence again.

'So where's your mum then?'

I took another bite of my apple, chewed and swallowed hard. 'Malawi,' I said.

We hadn't put the light on but the moon was so bright it lit the room.

'It's in…'

'…Africa,' he said. 'I know where Malawi is. What's she doing there?'

'You ask a lot of questions.'

'Fine, don't tell me then. I don't care.'

I hesitated. 'She's a nurse. She looks after sick kids with AIDs. Four years ago she dumped us to go out and look after them full time. I was eight.'

He stared at me but didn't speak.

'She sends me birthday and Christmas cards … sometimes.' I felt tears rise in my eyes and angrily brushed them away. 'She'll come back. I know she will. And she'll marry Dad again and…'

'Yeah, course she will. Your mum and my dad? A couple of prize-winning parents. Not!'

I threw my half-eaten apple at him as hard as I could.

He ducked.

It missed, bounced off the sofa and landed on Tia. In a panic she leapt onto Jago's lap. He cuddled her close.

'Sorry! Sorry!'

'S'okay.'

'Not you. I'm saying sorry to Tia.'

Carrying the little dog, he strode out through the French doors onto the balcony. After a minute I followed him. It was still warm. Bright stars filled the sky and the moon made a silver path across the sea.

Then he said it. 'Oh wow!' He was gazing up at the cliff top. 'That's the Shiver Stone, isn't it? I read up on it when I knew we were coming here. I can't wait to see it up close. Geology is my thing.'

'We could go tomorrow.'

He nodded. 'Yeah.'

We talked, staring out at the water, listening to the gentle washing sound of the waves.

'I'd like a dog. We've got five cats. They're okay but…'

'Yeah, cats are okay but not as good as a dog. So what's the story with your dad?'

He took a big breath in and blew it out again. 'Mum told you about him leaving. She tells everyone that. I wish she wouldn't. Anyway, Mum said he came home one night ten years ago, in a right panic and covered in blood. He packed a bag, kissed us goodbye and said he would get in touch when he could.'

'Covered in blood? Was he hurt?'

'Mum said it wasn't his blood.'

'Someone else's blood?'

'Someone else's blood,' Jago said.

We were silent while we thought about what that might mean. I shivered.

Tia struggled to get to me and Jago handed her over. She smelt sweet and warm. I stroked her tiny head.

'That was the last we saw of him. Until he was

on the telly after he did that statue thing on the beach. Mum nearly passed out when she saw him.'

'I took that video.'

'Yeah, you said.'

'I sneaked out at night and videoed him on my iPhone. Could have got myself grounded forever, but it was worth it.'

'Really?'

'Did you see me being interviewed about it on telly? I was on *Good Morning Wales*?'

'No.'

'Did you hear me on Radio Pembrokeshire, then? Talking to David Baker on the *Breakfast Show*?'

'No, I didn't. Sorry.'

I sighed.

He was eager to tell me the rest of his story. 'I don't know how Mum contacted him. She told me a few days ago we were going to a place called Carreg, in Pembrokeshire, to see my dad. Then he goes and runs off again. I don't care. I don't even know him. But Mum's really upset.'

'Candyfloss!' I shouted.

'What?'

'He bought candyfloss. Said it was for someone

special. That must have been you. He seemed happy, excited.'

Jago turned slowly towards me. 'So you don't think it was us he ran away from.'

'No. I think it was Skinny Beard.'

'Who?'

'He saw this man and he took off. Now this guy is looking for him. He said his name was Kemble Sykes – weird name.' So is Jago Pepper I thought, but I didn't say it.

'And this … Kemble, he's after my dad?'

'Yeah.' I yawned and glanced at the clock. 'It's three in the morning. I'm going back to bed.'

'Carys?'

'What?'

'That woman, Linette, you should be nicer to her.'

I was instantly angry. 'What's it got to do with you?'

'She loves you.'

'And what would you know about it?' I stormed off to my room.

CHAPTER 5

'Having her feet eaten by fish,' I said.

It was late the next morning and Dad had just asked where Linette was.

'What?'

I dipped the brush into the bottle of varnish and painted my big toenail yellow.

'What?' he repeated.

'It's her day off so she's gone for a fish pedicure at a beauty salon in Narberth. You stick your feet in a tank of water and these little fishes nibble away the dead skin. Gross.'

'If I'd known that's what she wanted I could have thrown her off the boat into a shoal of mackerel.'

I looked up, surprised. 'That's exactly what she said you'd say.'

Dad laughed and took a long swallow of his coffee. 'That woman knows me too well.'

Tia was asleep on the carpet making little snoring noises.

I painted the next toenail purple.

'I'm shattered. Been up all night. I'm off to bed.' Dad rubbed the bald spot on his head and looked around. 'Where's the boy?'

'Linette dropped him off at the hospital to see his mum. She's picking him up on the way back from her foot thing. They should be back soon.'

Just as I said that, we heard a key in the door and Linette came in with Jago. Dad gave her a hug. 'How's your mum?' he said to Jago.

Jago shrugged and looked away.

'Better, I think. Still looks a bit pale though,' Linette answered for him. She nodded at me. 'Madam here wouldn't come with us. Wanted to stay with the dog.' She saw what I was doing. 'Is that my nail polish, Carys?'

'No,' I lied.

'How many times do I have to tell you to leave my stuff alone!'

Dad closed his eyes and groaned. 'If you two are going to kick off again, I'm for my bed.'

He disappeared and Linette stormed into the kitchen. We could hear her banging pots and pans around.

'Thought we could go see if my dad is back yet,' Jago said.

'We'll take Tia.' I wiggled my toes in the air to dry the nail polish.

'Purple and yellow nails – looks like you've got foot fungus.' Jago screwed up his nose.

'Oh, thanks.'

'S'okay.' He smiled. I noticed his straight white teeth again and, embarrassed, ran my tongue across the metal wires covering mine.

He noticed. 'Lots of kids have those. It's almost a fashion accessory where I come from. The tin grin is in.'

That made me smile and for once I didn't close my lips to hide my brace.

It was hot and Tia panted up the hill, her tiny pink tongue lolling out of her mouth.

On the pavement there were several long stone tubs of flowers. Tia peed by every other one. The noise of cars and tourists faded as we made our way along the lane to Tristan's hut.

There was no answer to our knocks and, when we went inside, everything looked the same. I found a saucer and poured cold water into it for Tia. She lapped it up noisily.

Disappointed, Jago flopped onto the sofa. 'I don't get it. Do you think he knows what happened to my mum?'

I shrugged. Tia was sniffing at something she'd found on the floor.

I bent down and picked up an orange tic tac. You know when you read in a book sometimes, 'The hairs on the back on my neck stood up'? That's what happened right then. There was this crawly feeling between my shoulder blades and I spun round half expecting Skinny Beard to be standing right behind me.

'He's been in here.'

'My dad?'

'No, the guy who's after him.' I showed Jago the sweet in my palm.

He looked puzzled.

'He eats orange tic tacs all the time.'

'My dad does?'

'No! Kemble Sykes. He's been in here looking for your dad. He must really want to find him. Look, there's no point hanging around. Let's drop Tia home and go to the beach for the afternoon. We can try again later.'

Halfway down the lane, Tia looked up at the window of the guesthouse called Seaview and growled. A curtain twitched and someone peered down at us.

I punched Jago's arm and pointed up. 'There, there he is. That's the man, the one after your dad.'

But the figure pulled back into the room before Jago saw him.

'I don't think it's a coincidence him staying right there, so close to your dad's place, do you? He's definitely stalking him.'

Before Jago could answer, Tia gave a sharp bark and jerked at the lead so hard it pulled out of my hand. She hurtled up the long path to Hug

Howells' house with the lead trailing. I chased after her, calling her name, but she completely ignored me. When she reached the door, she scrabbled frantically to be let in.

Panting, I reached her just as the door opened a few inches and the enormous Hug Howells, her face red and angry, stood barring the way.

'Get that damn dog off my property!' she shouted.

'But I...'

'You heard me. It's nothing but a nuisance. Bad enough I have to put up with that sculptor bloke, not paying his rent, parking his motorbike in front of my garage.'

I grabbed Tia's lead and took a few steps back.

I didn't know Hug Howells well, but she'd always seemed like a nice person before. She made honey from her bees. 'Hug's Happy Honey' was in all the local shops – bright yellow jars with a cartoon of a cross-eyed bee on the label. Linette sold them in the Crab's Claw.

She was still ranting about Tia. 'Bringing that yappy little pest here, making a racket. Get off my property, will you!'

'She's not a pest,' I shouted at the closing door. I

hauled Tia back down the path. She was still tugging, trying to get to Hug's house.

Jago was waiting at the gate. 'What was all that about?'

'Seems Hug hates dogs.' I didn't say it sounded like she hated Tristan too.

'Hug? That's her name?'

'She was called Caress when she was born. But Dad said she got so big and strong when she was a kid everyone said she was more like a Bear Hug than a Caress. Hug stuck.'

'Nasty piece of work.' Jago frowned.

I nodded but it didn't feel right. Dad told me that, when Mum went, Hug left a jar of honey on our doorstep every week for months and months.

'Come on. Let's drop Tia home for a while and go to the beach.'

'What about the Shiver Stone? You said we could go there. I'd rather do that. I'm not much of a swimmer.'

'We can do that later. It's not going anywhere. Let's get to the beach first while it's still hot. I'll teach you to dive off the cliff.'

'Cliff? Okay, I'll get my hammer, it's in my backpack in the caravan,' he said.

I looked at him like he'd gone mad. He explained on the way home.

'Geology?'

'Yes.'

'Like rocks and stuff?'

'Yes. Carreg has got some unique folding.'

I had no idea what 'folding' was and he drivelled on about something called anthracite and ammonoids. 'The Shiver Stone is probably...'

I was losing interest fast. 'Don't you get into trouble at school having your hair so long?' I said to change the subject.

'What? No. I mean I don't go to school. Mum home schools me.'

'Cool,' I said.

'Not always.'

We made our way through the usual press of holidaymakers. It took a while – everyone wanted to pat Tia and say how cute she was. We were close to the caravan site that Jago and his mum had booked into.

But, to get there, we had to go through one of the Troll Holes. And I hated them.

The Troll Holes are really three tunnels

between Carreg and Wiseman's Bridge. They were dug out of the cliff ages ago to move trucks of coal. There's loads of old mine workings around here. The tunnels are dark and damp and when I was only four, a ten-year-old neighbour thought it would be funny to scare the hell out of me. I can remember even now what he said...

'They're Troll Holes, Carys. Trolls are huge ugly things with claws and sharp teeth. They're invisible. They hide in the Troll Holes until small kids come in and then they grab them and eat them.'

Dad said I had nightmares for weeks. And now, stupid as it is, they still scare me. I always run through as fast as I can. That's okay in the short one but in the longer ones you can't see the light at the end and I've slipped over more than once. I hate them. I always go around the beach way if the tide is out, but I didn't want Jago to know that.

He wanted to go through the tunnels – thought they were cool. He rabbited on about the rock formation. He was so busy trying to tell me how metamorphic rocks were created, he didn't see me hesitate before I plunged in.

I picked up Tia and cuddled her to give me

courage. Jago's voice echoed off the cold stone. I held my breath and counted slowly to distract myself.

At last we were out in the bright sunshine of Coppet Hall Beach.

'I've done a lot of research on this place,' Jago said. 'Did you know that Coppet Hall comes from the words Coal Pit Hall?'

'Course I did,' I said.

I didn't. And, I thought maybe I should do a bit of research on Carreg. It was annoying having a stranger tell you things about your own home.

Jago's caravan was nice. The curtains were half closed, so it was cool and shaded inside. It had everything: little shower room, fridge, microwave, and a TV. They hadn't had time to use it and their stuff was still packed. Jago rummaged through a blue backpack and pulled out a small hammer, goggles and some other bits and pieces.

He arranged them neatly on the floor, naming them as he did. 'Rock pick, collection bag…'

I think he was trying to impress me. He didn't.

'Come on. Get your swimming costume and let's get to the beach.'

I'd slipped Tia off the lead and looked in the cupboards for a saucer or something to give her a drink of water.

It was a while before I noticed that she wasn't in the caravan anymore. The door was open and Tia was gone.

I panicked. Raced outside into the heat and blinding light of the day.

'Tia! Tia! Here, girl. Tia!'

The caravan site was almost deserted; everyone was at the beach. I saw a couple with two small children trailing buckets and spades and ran towards them.

'Have you seen a dog? A little dog?'

They shook their heads.

Jago ran in the other direction shouting for Tia at the top of his lungs.

I climbed onto a hedge and scanned the site. White caravans stood in neat rows. Most of them with wet costumes and towels fluttering from the windows.

I couldn't see Tia anywhere. I felt the sting of tears in my eyes.

I bolted across Coppet Hall car park and headed for the tunnel. I could see Jago threading his way through people on the beach – searching and calling her name.

Before I knew it I was in darkness. The cold stone chilled me like a shower of water. I pushed past people, ignoring angry comments. 'A dog? Have you seen a little dog?' My voice rang out in the damp vault of the tunnel.

Then, in the arch of bright light at the far end, I saw a silhouette. Someone running, cradling something in their arms, a baby, or maybe a small dog?

I rushed after her, out of the tunnel and into the sunshine.

Tia heard my shout and immediately struggled so violently that the woman dropped her. Tia ran to me and leapt into my arms.

Relief made me weak. I sank to the floor burying my face in Tia's fur.

The woman was watching me, a strange look on her face. 'I just found her wandering around … I, um … thought I'd better take her to the police.'

'Thank you, thank you so much, I thought we'd lost her. I don't understand it, she's never wandered off before. She's usually quite clingy, like a little limpet.' I knew I was gabbling but was so relieved I couldn't stop.

The woman didn't laugh, didn't even smile, she just stared. 'Yes, well, I'd better get going.' She blinked and pushed her glasses back up onto the bridge of her nose.

Again she gave me a strange look but just then Jago rushed up looking as happy as I felt.

'You found her.' He was gasping for breath and his long blonde hair was wet with sweat.

'Well, it wasn't me. It was this lady who…'

But the woman was walking away towards Carreg. Walking fast.

I shrugged. 'Don't ever do that to me again, Tia, will you?' I stroked her soft head and she tucked her nose under my chin.

Jago had her lead and he clipped it onto her collar. 'We don't want to lose you again, do we?' he said.

Tia licked his hand.

'I thought for a minute there we'd have to tell my dad we'd lost his dog.' Then he added quickly, 'When he comes back.'

I was beginning to wonder if Tristan was ever coming back.

CHAPTER
6

We were nearly home before I realised that, for the first time ever, I'd run through a Troll Hole without being scared. I was pretty chuffed about that.

We made tuna sandwiches and took one down to Dad in his shed. I told him about Hug Howells shouting at me.

'Can't believe it. Hug is as sweet as her honey. She might look like an all-in wrestler but I've always found her such a gentle soul. Hand me that glue?'

I passed Dad the tube and he squirted a thin line along a piece of wood. He was making yet another birdhouse. I think he's on a mission to give free homes to all the birds in Carreg.

The shed was filled with the smell of clean wood and glue. Curls of shavings littered the floor and the air was thick with sawdust.

'Well, Hug wasn't sweet earlier, was she?' I looked at Jago for backup and he shook his head.

'Can we leave Tia with you for a while? We want to go to the beach.'

'Sure. If you take the stuff out of that cardboard box and put something soft in it she can have a nap.'

'You, um … you'd better keep her tied up if you're going to be in and out of the shed.'

Dad raised his eyebrows. 'She might run off?'

I shot Jago a warning look. I didn't think it was a good idea to tell Dad we'd lost her once already. He might think Tia should have someone more responsible looking after her.

'Just in case,' I said.

'She'd be better off in the flat but old Mrs Jenkins in number three is already sniffing around and complaining. I told her it was only for a day or two but…' Dad said.

'I know. I know. No dogs allowed in the flats. You keep telling me.'

'Don't think we can have her in the caravan when Mum comes out of hospital either. There's a "no pets" sign by the entrance,' Jago said. 'Just wish my dad would come back...' His head drooped and his long hair covered his face.

On the way to the beach Jago suddenly decided we should go to the police and make a missing persons report.

'And say what?' I said. 'That your dad has gone away for a day?'

'It's nearly two days now, and there's that guy you told me about. The one who's stalking him. I think Dad's in real danger. Remember, he was covered in blood on the night he ran away from Bristol. Maybe there was a ... a ... murder or something.'

I thought for a minute. The idea of murder had crossed my mind too, but stuff like that doesn't happen to ordinary people – does it? It was more likely Tristan had been in some sort of fight or an accident. But then again, what did we really know about him? He was secretive...

'Wouldn't hurt to report him missing, I suppose,' I agreed.

The police officer at the desk didn't look much older than us. He was skinny with sticky-up hair and an Adam's apple the size of a walnut.

He took our names and addresses, but when we told him what happened his forehead wrinkled. 'One day? One day?'

'He wouldn't run off and leave his dog unless it was something serious,' I said.

Another police officer came out from an inner office. 'Hello, you're Dai Thomas' daughter, aren't you? Carys?'

I nodded.

'What can I do for you?'

We told her the same story.

'So you're the son of our celebrity sculptor? I can see the likeness,' she said to Jago.

She turned to me. 'Tell you what, I'll give your dad a ring later and find out a bit more. You just leave it with me.'

The young police officer turned to his boss. His Adam's apple bobbed up and down furiously. 'One day, ma'am,' he said, 'he's only been gone one day.'

'I said leave this with me,' she said, sternly.

There was nothing else we could do so we left.

We trudged through warm sand, dodging beach balls, running kids and people carrying ice creams from the van parked near the water's edge. The sun shone bright and hot and the beach was crowded.

'Keep going,' I said. 'When we get around that headland it'll be much quieter and we should have the place to ourselves.'

Jago grumbled, but it was worth the hike and the scramble up and over hot boulders.

The entrance to the cave was dark and cool and the water-washed pebbles gleamed. It's a secret place tucked into a corner of the cliffs and hidden from the main beach when the tide is in. The sea rushed and gushed and formed a deep gulley between the cave and the rocks.

Directly above, the Shiver Stone stands, looking proudly out over Carmarthen Bay.

Dad brought me here all the time when I was a small kid. It was our secret place. Not many visitors bothered to make the climb, not when they had lovely sandy beaches within easy reach.

'Now, watch this,' I said. I pulled off my t-shirt and shorts and kicked off my flip-flops. Adjusting the straps of my swimming costume, I took a deep breath and began to climb.

Small flint stones dug into my feet as I clambered up to the ledge on the cliff below the Shiver Stone.

A gull screeched a warning before launching off its perch into the clear blue sky. Below me the sea glittered in shades of green. A strong breeze whipped my hair around my face.

'Can you see me?' I hollered down to Jago.

He waved, shielding his eyes from the sun with his other hand.

'Ready?'

As always, I heard Dad's voice in my mind.

Bend your knees.

Extend your arms above your head, overlap your hands and lock your thumbs together.

Keep your arms pressed tight against your ears.

Bend at the waist.

Jump!

And with a shriek of, 'Woooohoooo,' I dived off the cliff.

I felt the wild rush of air before…

…the ice-cold impact of the sea.

And then, the slice through and down into the silence and up again to bubble-burst through the surface into the warmth and noise and light.

I laughed out loud and I swam in short, strong strokes to where Jago stood open mouthed on the rocks.

'Awesome,' he said.

He looked funny in his red swimming trunks – too thin and too white. He'd threaded a shell into his long hair and I wasn't sure if it looked cool or stupid so I didn't mention it.

I stumbled towards him across the pebbles. 'Ow. Ouch. Ow! Take a video of me on your mobile, will you? I want to check something.'

'I haven't got a mobile.'

'No mobile?'

'They fry your brains.'

'That's what your dad says.'

Jago smiled, and I could see he was pleased he had something in common with his father.

'You look a lot like him, too,' I added and the smile turned into a huge grin.

'Here. Use my phone. Press this button to focus.'

'You're going to do it again?'

'Yeah, I wasn't too happy with my entry that time,' I lied.

The truth was I knew I was good. I was in the school diving team and had competed for Pembrokeshire. I'd won a load of trophies and medals too. Yes, I knew I was good and I liked people to see just how good.

Jago videoed my next three dives but he was getting bored. The funny little hammer came out and he put on the goggles which made him look a real nerd.

I wondered what my friend, Becca, would make of him.

He tapped at the cliff face and mumbled geology words I'd never heard of.

I lay on my towel on a flat boulder to dry off and doze in the sun. I closed my eyes. I was tired from lack of sleep the night before and the gentle drag and pull of pebbles and sea was such a relaxing sound.

'Did you know it was my dad?'

'What?'

Jago's shadow blocked out the sun. I flicked my hand at him to tell him to move aside.

'The sculptures on the beach thing?'

I sat up. 'Oh that. No, not at first. He was my first guess obviously, being a sculptor – he was everyone's first guess. But he said it was nothing to do with him and he had better things to do than play silly pranks. He's a good liar. Oh, no offence.'

Jago shrugged.

'So you just decided you'd sneak out in the middle of the night and catch The Stone Man. Is that what they called him?'

'That's what the papers called him. I preferred The Phantom Sculptor.' I laughed, lay back down and closed my eyes.

'So, what, it started off in the local newspapers…?'

I sighed and sat up. I wasn't going to get a nap, that was obvious.

'It started one morning when someone noticed a pile of stones arranged like a tower on the beach. It started simple but got more complicated and more amazing. All sorts of things made out of stones and pebbles and bits of driftwood. They were awesome. Look. I've got pictures on my phone.'

I passed my mobile and showed him how to scroll through.

He shielded the screen and took his time looking at every one.

I rubbed more sunscreen on and lay down again.

Eventually Jago handed the phone back to me. 'It was a pretty cool thing to do, wasn't it?' he said.

'Yes. And your mum saw my video? And the bit on telly where they identified him?'

'Yes.'

I thought for a minute. 'Do you think that's where this Kemble Sykes saw him too?'

'Maybe.'

Something else had been going around in my mind. 'Do you know what *Vulpes Vulpes* means?'

He shook his head and the shell in his hair swung round and hit him in the teeth. It must have hurt but he pretended not to notice.

'It's tattooed on your dad's arm. The weird thing is it's tattooed on Kemble Sykes' arm too. It must be a secret club or something. Your dad wouldn't tell me what it meant when I asked him.'

Jago shook his head again. This time he'd grabbed hold of the shell in his hair so it wouldn't swing round and hit him in the face.

'Okay, one more dive,' I said.

Jago sighed. 'Do you want me to video you again?'

'Course.'

He held my phone up towards the cliff, squinting through the viewer.

'She's still there,' he said.

'Who?'

'Some woman. She's behind that boulder. She's been watching us with binoculars.'

I had no objections to an audience.

'This dive will be the best one yet,' I said.

The breeze was stronger and it stole the heat out of the day. A cloud passed across the sun and I shivered. I took a deep breath and stood still and tall, my feet inching off the ledge.

I stared out at the sea, focused and went through the motions in my head.

Bend your knees.

Extend your arms...

But this time, as I jumped, I felt my ankle twist beneath me. I struggled in mid-air, trying to straighten my body, but the water came up too fast.

I felt my legs arch to the left and then the hard

smack and sting of pain as I entered the water. Instead of a neat splash the water crashed around me.

When I surfaced this time I wasn't smiling.

Jago was.

'That was rubbish,' he said, handing me my towel.

'I slipped.'

'Yeah, well, still rubbish.'

My ankle hurt where it had twisted and my legs were red and burning. It was a rubbish dive and I was angry with myself.

'Like to see you do better.' I pushed him once, hard. He tumbled off the rocks, slipping and sliding on the seaweed and, with a cry, fell headlong into the deep gulley of water.

He came up struggling and thrashing and trying to shout something, but a wave splashed into his mouth and he went under again.

I was laughing so hard I almost fell in myself.

The second time he surfaced, coughing and choking, I stopped laughing.

'Can't swim,' he gasped.

In a flash I was in the water beside him, but he was struggling and fighting in panic.

He went under again and I felt the same panic tighten my chest.

'Get to the rocks.'

I tried pushing him, but his flailing arms hit me in the face. He was stronger and taller and wild with fear. I managed to steer him to the cliff edge but a wave washed over us and I saw the terror in his eyes.

Again and again he grabbed at the rocks, but they were slippery with seaweed and sharp with limpet shells. The struggling and thrashing was making him weak.

Panicking, I screamed at him, 'Grab on and pull yourself up, for God's sake!'

'I can't! I can't!'

Another wave crashed in and his face disappeared in a wild spray of froth and foam. I heard him splutter and, when he came up again, he had drifted further away.

I started shouting. 'Help! Help!' But in my heart I knew that even if someone heard me it would take too long to climb over the headland and down to the tiny inlet where the waves were growing stronger as Jago grew weaker.

CHAPTER

7

A wave swelled behind Jago and I saw, with a thudding heart, that it would carry him towards the mouth of the cave. If I could get out and...

I scrambled onto dry land. Every inch of my body trembled with exertion and fright. What if he drowns? What if he drowns? The thought pounded in my head. In seconds I was at the cave entrance.

I splashed desperately through the water searching for Jago. I saw a flash of red swimming trucks. Grabbing his thrashing arm, I clung on tight. He tried to pull himself out, but the pebbles under his feet were rolling and shifting with the underwater current – he couldn't stand. It was like a tug of war between the sea and us as the force of the tide tried to drag him back out. A tug of war we were losing. Jago's hair was slicked dark against his white face. He was spitting out water, retching and coughing.

I felt him slip away from me. I gritted my teeth, heaving backwards with all my strength.

From nowhere, a hand stretched down and grasped him by the hair. 'Quick! Now pull!'

Together we dragged him out and he crumpled, trembling, on the rocks.

I collapsed beside him and we lay flat out on our backs, panting, gasping and shuddering.

At last Jago raised himself on his elbows. 'You pushed me in.' He was furious.

'How was I to know you can't swim! You said earlier that you weren't much of a swimmer. You didn't say you couldn't swim at all. I don't know anyone who can't swim. It's like saying you can't breathe!'

'You should have checked before you pushed me in!'

'I pulled you out!'

'You wouldn't have had to pull me out if you hadn't PUSHED ME IN!'

We were both shouting so loud it was a surprise when a quiet voice behind us said, 'Hey, hey, it's okay now. Everything's okay, no harm done.'

We turned and saw the woman leaning against a boulder. She looked strangely familiar.

'Yeah, well, no thanks to her. If you hadn't been here…' Jago was too mad to even finish what he was saying.

'It's just lucky I happened to be passing,' she said.

He scraped his long hair out of his eyes, twisting it and wringing the water out with his hands. 'But you weren't.' Jago was staring at her.

She was drying off her shorts with a towel and stopped to look up.

'What?'

He narrowed his eyes against the sun. 'You weren't just passing. You were up there watching us with binoculars.'

The woman's face blushed deep red right up to the roots of her short black hair.

'I don't know what you mean. I was bird-watching when I heard you shouting and … and…'

'Lucky for us you were,' I said.

Jago suddenly went into a coughing fit.

'I've got a drink here,' the woman said.

She took a bottle of water from a bag and handed it to Jago. He nodded his thanks and drank quickly, swallowing hard.

'That's the salt water I expect,' she said. 'It'll make your throat sore for a while.'

As she turned around we both saw it.

She wore only a bikini top and shorts and it ran deep and red and ugly down her spine like a snake. It was a shock against her white skin. A scar – a scar as thick as my finger running from her neck all the way down her back.

When she saw us staring, I looked away, embarrassed.

Jago didn't.

'What happened to your back?' His voice was croaky and he coughed to clear his throat.

'An accident,' she said, 'a long time ago when I was a kid. I needed a lot of surgery. Couldn't walk for a while.'

She pulled a t-shirt out from her bag and hastily put it on, covering the scar.

She didn't seem in any hurry to leave. She brought out a packet of Oreos. I was suddenly hungry and took three.

Jago shook his head. 'Throat still sore,' he said.

He went to hand the water back to her, but she said, 'Keep it.'

And that's when I recognised her. She'd been wearing different clothes and glasses I think, but it was her all right.

'You're the woman in the Troll Hole.' The Troll Hole bit came out by accident. I quickly changed my words. 'The tunnel, I mean. It was you who found Tia this morning, wasn't it?'

'Tia?'

'Our dog, well, his dad's dog.'

For a minute I thought she was going to deny it. She hesitated and then gave an odd laugh.

'Oh was that your little dog? How strange we should meet again. And where is the dear little thing now?'

'At home in the shed with Dad.'

'A shed doesn't seem like a safe place to keep a dog who likes to run away.'

'If he has to leave her for a minute or two he'll make sure she's tied with her lead but, like I said, she doesn't usually run off. We can't have her in the flat. No dogs allowed. We sneak her in at night though. She's safe on my bed then.' I thought for a minute. 'You rescued Tia and Jago today.'

'Didn't need rescuing,' Jago mumbled.

I was going to have something to say about that, but just then a shower of stones tumbled down from above.

We all looked up to see a group of people leaning over the cliff edge near the Shiver Stone.

'They need to get back from there. It's really dangerous,' I said.

'I saw you dive from not that far below,' the woman answered, still looking up at the top of the cliff.

'My dad dived off the top, off Shiver Stone ridge, when he was only thirteen. The youngest kid in the village to do it, ever. Not many adults have managed it. One guy, a tourist, tried a few years back and ended up paralysed. It's too scary for me.'

'The Shiver Stone, is that its name? It's an impressive rock. There's something spiritual in these stones. I live near the stone circles of Avebury. They're quite magical. If I'm frightened or worried I speak to the stones – they always help me. They're my friends.'

She was staring up at the Shiver Stone and it was like she'd forgotten we were there. Her voice went all floaty. 'The stones are places of death and sacrifice,' she said, 'timeless, motionless…'

She was starting to creep me out and, when I looked at Jago, he rolled his eyes at me.

'Um, guess we'd better be going now. Thank you for – you know, for all the rescuing and stuff,' I said.

'What?' She shivered, as if waking up out of a dream. 'Oh, it was nothing. I'd better be off too. Back to my birdwatching.'

She slung a pair of binoculars around her neck and started the climb up over the headland. Before she was out of sight she turned and gave a short wave.

We waved back.

'Freeeeaky,' I said.

'I'm cold now and I want to go home,' Jago moaned. We crawled over the rocks to the other side where our clothes and things were scattered across a boulder. Jago grabbed his jeans and t-shirt and pulled them on roughly before packing his geology stuff away.

'Lucky she was here though,' he finally admitted. He dragged his wet hair back into a ponytail. It made him look different.

I inspected a graze on my knee. Then got dressed too.

'That woman, there's something...' I didn't get to finish my sentence. My mobile gave its message ping. I picked it up and peered at the screen. There were five missed calls from Dad and three texts:

Carys & Jago, come home right away!

Carys & Jago, come home now!

COME HOME!

CHAPTER 8

We were up and over the rocks in no time. It was about five in the afternoon so there were fewer people on the beach. It still felt like a crowd though as we raced across the sand, skirting windbreaks, sandcastles and families huddled in groups.

I was amazed at how quickly Jago had recovered. 'It could be Tia,' I shouted to him. 'Maybe she's missing again!'

'It's not Tia. It's my mum. Something's happened to my mum. I know it has.' Jago's face was grim, almost angry. There was no point arguing with him.

I thought I was pretty fast, but Jago was ahead of me, his long legs pumping. We twisted in and out of traffic and hurtled along the pavement ignoring angry comments from idling holiday-makers.

Dad was waiting for us at the gate. 'It's your mum, Jago. She's had a relapse. Let's get you to the hospital.'

I sat in the waiting room with Dad while Jago went into his mother.

'Dylan called from the hospital. He said she was having problems breathing. It can happen sometimes after anaphylactic shock apparently. Poor woman, she's really going through it.' Dad was whispering, which made it seem more frightening, more serious.

Jago is going through it as well, I thought. I decided now wasn't a good time to tell Dad I'd almost drowned him.

There were only three other people in the waiting room. We sat on orange plastic chairs arranged in two lines, facing each other. A phone rang somewhere in another room.

A nurse called out a name and a man left, leaving an eerie quiet. Someone dropped a magazine. My bathing costume was still damp under my clothes, and so uncomfortable it made me wriggle.

Feeling thirsty, I got up and helped myself to a paper cup. The gurgling the water cooler made sounded so loud I said sorry to no one in particular.

We waited for what seemed like ages but was probably only twenty minutes or so. At last the doctor, Dad's friend, came out to speak to us.

He was smiling. I blew out my breath in relief.

'She's okay now. We had some quite serious breathing problems for a while there. How are you fixed for looking after her son for another night or so, Dai?'

'No problem,' Dad said. 'Isn't there someone we should be contacting, though – family, friends?'

'The boy says not. Says he and his mother are on their own mostly. What about the boy's father – no sign of him yet?'

Dad shook his head.

'Someone's been calling several times a day to find out how Polly is, a woman. She won't leave her name but sounds local. Any ideas who that could be?'

Dad looked puzzled. 'No,' he said.

Dr Dylan spoke quietly to Dad. 'This whole thing is becoming a bit of a mystery. What do you think is going on?'

Dad rubbed his bald patch. 'Beats me,' he said.

'Hmm. You two can go and see her now if you want,' Dr Dylan said.

Walking into her room, I thought Polly would be angry with me. Jago must have told her I pushed him into the sea.

I felt my face burn. I was wrong, though, because she tried to smile.

At some point during the day she'd drawn her eyebrows back on, but drawn them crookedly. One of them had to avoid the stitches so it was a different shape. It gave her an odd look. While her mouth was smiling, her forehead was frowning. Very weird.

'Hi,' she said.

'Linette says she'll pop round later, after work, with some shampoo and stuff,' Dad said. He looked and sounded awkward, standing at the bottom of the bed rubbing his big fisherman's hands together. 'Your boy is more than welcome to stay with us for a bit longer. As long as you need, in fact,' he added, quickly.

Jago was sitting by the bed holding his mother's hand. He didn't look up. The salt water had dried in his hair and it looked like a bird's nest. I realised my brown, tangled frizz probably looked ten times worse.

Polly nodded weakly. 'I don't know how to thank you, Dai, and you too, Carys – and Linette, of course. You've all been so kind.' She started to cry. 'Oh, and thank you for the flowers, too.'

Dad looked really embarrassed. 'Flowers? Not from us, I'm afraid. Right. Well, if there's nothing we can do for the minute, I'll get Carys home. Jago, do you want to stay with your mum for a bit longer? Linette can pick you up later when she drops in the stuff.'

'Yeah.' Jago's voice sounded strange and I realized he was trying not to cry. He didn't look at me.

Dad hates hospitals, they make him nervous, so we left as soon as we could. As we crossed the car park I thought I saw a figure dart quickly behind the wall. It was an odd thing for someone to do – suspicious.

While Dad was searching for his car keys I wandered down to where the ambulance was parked and leaned over the hedge, trying to see around the trees. There was no one there. I wondered if whoever was hiding from us knew where Tristan was and why he'd disappeared.

While Dad made his famous fishfinger and ketchup sandwiches, I took Tia for a walk along the road. People kept stopping me to make a fuss of her and say how cute she was, but I wasn't in the mood to talk. Not even about Tia. I had a lot on my mind.

So much had happened in the last couple of days. Tristan running away, Polly's bee sting, Hug Howells screaming at me, Jago nearly drowning. Then there was Kemble Sykes. What was he after? Why was he so desperate to find Tristan? And most importantly – where was Tristan?

Dad was fishing again that night, so Linette was staying at our flat. She'd brought Jago back from the hospital.

'Pizza or fish cakes?'

'Chicken pie,' I said. Linette frowned at me but took three pies out of the freezer.

'Peas or sweetcorn?'

'Yes,' I said.

'Ah, right. We're in one of those moods, are we, Madam?'

'I'm not. I don't know about you.' I turned the telly up.

Jago was sitting on the sofa with Tia on his lap. 'How did you get her into the flat without Mrs Jenkins seeing?' I asked.

'Hid her in my geology bag.'

We both laughed. I was glad he wasn't still mad at me for nearly drowning him.

Telly was boring, so after dinner Jago and I watched a DVD – the DVD was boring too.

We took Tia out onto the balcony, where she promptly peed on the new pot plant Linette had brought round. I didn't stop her.

About ten o'clock, Linette said she was going to bed and for us to remember to put the lights out.

It was cool on the balcony. Lights from the flats along the beachfront shone in squares on the sand. A group of people had lit a fire on the beach and we could hear their laughter and smell sausages frying. The sea swooshed gently. Waves left a fringe of foam on the sand.

Now that we were on our own I felt awkward. 'So what does your mum do?' I said, to make conversation.

'She's a Kirlian photographer.'

'What's a Kir ... Kir...?'

'Kirlian photographer. She takes pictures of people's auras.'

'Auras? Like a kind of light glowing around you? My friend Becca is into that. She says good people have nice-coloured auras and horrible people have grotty ones.'

'Yeah. If you have the right equipment you can take pictures. There are auras around rocks and trees and stuff too.'

A sudden cheer from below made Jago stand and look over the balcony to see what the people on the beach were doing. I thought again how much he looked like his father with that long silver-blond hair down over his shoulders.

He sat back down and carried on talking. 'We go to music festivals. You know Glastonbury, places like that.'

'How does she take pictures of auras?'

'Special camera, something to do with electricity, then Mum reads them. She can tell what that person is like, or how they're feeling, by the mix of colours and where they are on the body.'

I thought about that for a minute.

Jago nodded towards the Shiver Stone. 'I want to go there tomorrow, for sure. Think I've had enough swimming to last me a while.'

I changed the subject quickly in case we were heading for the 'You pushed me in' argument again. 'Do you know the story of the Shiver Stone?' I asked him.

'I think that, probably, like Stonehenge, the Stones were...'

'Nooooo. I mean the story, the legend, the myth. Do you want to hear it?'

'Yeah. But first, have you got any crisps or anything? The smell of those sausages cooking is making me hungry.'

I went to the kitchen, filled a bowl with salted peanuts and grabbed two bags of cheesy Wotsits. I brought two cans of coke too.

He'd collected cushions to sit on and the duvet

off the sofa bed which we folded over our knees. Tia immediately snuggled into my lap.

There was a click, fizz as Jago tugged the ring pull. He took a big slurp of coke, staring out over the sea.

'Right,' he said.

I dropped a cheesy Wotsit onto my lap in front of Tia's nose. She sniffed it and then licked at it gently.

'Okay,' I said. 'A long, long time ago lived a…'

Jago snorted with laughter and coke came out of his nose. He coughed and brushed at his t-shirt.

'If you're gonna laugh, then…'

'No. Sorry, sorry,' he said. 'Go on, a long, long time ago…'

He popped a handful of peanuts in his mouth. I waited for him to chew and swallow.

The group on the beach was getting really noisy, having races and pushing each other over. Their shouts and laughter drifted out to sea.

'I won't interrupt any more. Tell me the story, please?' he said.

So I did. And, immediately, my mind went back in time. I was five again and my mother lay in bed with me, telling me the story as we stared out through the rain at the Shiver Stone. I remember the scent of her perfume – it's called Anaïs Anaïs and smells like flowers. I keep the empty bottle on my dressing table.

'King Cynwrig was a fierce soldier king who ruled Pembrokeshire.

'Pembrokeshire was under siege from many enemies, who wanted to conquer the beautiful county, but the fiercest was the Seawitch. She would attack under cover of a storm and create havoc in the towns and villages along the coast. King Cynwrig had twenty sons and, when he left to fight somewhere else, he'd leave his sons to guard the coastline.

'Owain, his youngest son, was put in charge of Carreg.

'"Never leave your post," his father told him. "If the Seawitch attacks, light the bonfire to warn the people to get out of their houses before she destroys them with her storms."

'On the very first night, Owain stood guard on the cliff top as the village of Carreg went to sleep. All was in darkness. Owain wasn't the bravest son and already felt frightened.

'At midnight the temperature suddenly dropped. Dark clouds covered the moon. Rain, rippling the surface of the calm sea, drifted towards Owain. He shivered and pulled his cloak tighter around his body.

'Then lightning blazed the sky. The rain whipped down like nails and as the sea swelled, boats in the harbour heaved and tossed in the rising tide. Waves lashed the harbour wall. The brine hissed and lashed Owain's face. He tried to raise the alarm, but shook so much he couldn't light the bonfire. A mountainous wave rose up before him. As it receded Owain saw the Seawitch's face in the sky where the moon should be. It was a mask of hatred. She looked down on Owain, opened her massive mouth and roared her terrible scream. Owain was terrified. He shook so much he dropped the burning torch over the cliff – and then he ran. Many people died that night crushed in their homes by the Seawitch's storm.

'The king was so furious with his cowardly son that, with one stroke of his sword, he turned him to stone. "You'll never run away again. You'll stay on the cliff top guarding Carreg forever," he said.'

I brought my voice down to a whisper. 'And they say, if there is danger near, and you touch the stone – it will shiver as poor Owain tries to warn you – with his fear.'

'Wow. That was pretty cool.' Jago snuggled down into the duvet and lay his head on a cushion.

Tia sniffed at my bag of cheesy Wotsits and I gave her one.

'The Shiver Stone is special to me and Dad too,' I said quietly. 'After Mum left I had nightmares. Dad had to go out fishing at night sometimes and leave me with a sitter. He told me, if I woke from a bad dream, to tell it to the Shiver Stone. He said that, out at sea, he'd hear me and send his love back. I knew it wasn't true, of course. But talking to Dad through the Shiver Stone, when I was scared or upset, helped.'

The party crowd on the beach had gone quiet. Someone was playing a guitar and singing. It was a soft, sad song and it floated through the air up to where we sat.

I rubbed at the tears on my cheeks and flicked my hand towards the people on the beach. 'Sad song, huh?'

But Jago was fast asleep.

I got up slowly, cuddling Tia in my arms, and went to bed.

'Get up, Carys, it's gone nine and I have to get to work.' Linette was tugging at my duvet.

'And?' I tried to snuggle back down.

'And I told your dad I'd make sure you had a proper breakfast before I go to the Crab Claw.'

'I can make my own breakfast, thank you.' I turned my face to the pillow.

'Get up, Carys!'

She suddenly lunged forward and sniffed at me. 'Is that my perfume you're wearing? I've told you before...'

Anger shot through me, an anger so strong and sudden I sat bolt upright in bed and shouted, 'Get out! Get out of my room. Get out of our house. Me and Dad don't need you here. We don't want you here. You with your stupid cartoon hair!'

I was screaming. Tia shot off my bed in panic and scrabbled at the door to get out.

Linette had jerked back sharply at my first shout and now stood leaning against the wall, obviously shaken.

I glared at her, my eyes narrowed, my heart pounding.

I thought Linette was going to cry. 'You can be a real brat sometimes, Carys Thomas,' she said quietly.

She opened the door and standing right outside was my dad – looking angrier than I've ever seen him, ever.

CHAPTER
9

'Get dressed and get out here, Carys. Now!'

Dad doesn't do mad. I can't remember him even telling me off really. The last time I saw him close to angry was on my eleventh birthday when there was nothing from my mum, not even a card.

I'd asked him for the hundredth time if Mum's present had arrived when he suddenly slammed his fist into what was left of my birthday cake. He looked astonished at what he'd done. He said he was sorry, over and over, and held me tight.

Afterwards, he stood staring out to sea for a long, long time.

I got dressed as slowly as I could and went into the lounge. Dad was on the balcony talking to Jago. Tia was on Jago's lap. Linette had gone to the café.

I slouched over and dropped down onto a chair. I began texting Becca.

'Jago, I wonder if you'd take Tia for a walk? I need to have a little chat with Carys.' The words 'little chat' didn't sound good.

Jago clipped on Tia's lead and left without a word.

Dad didn't hang about. As soon as the door closed he turned to me. 'Don't you ever let me hear you speak to anyone that way again, Carys. Do you understand?'

I nodded slowly but kept texting.

'Put that phone down.'

I kept texting.

Dad lunged across the table and snatched the phone out of my hand. 'This is confiscated for two weeks and so is your laptop. When Linette comes around this evening I expect a full apology from you.' He was breathing heavily. 'Do you understand?' He said each word loudly, clearly.

'Why are you sticking up for her? We don't need her here. We were fine on our own before she came.'

I grabbed my bag and tore off through the door, slamming it behind me. Racing down the steps, I nearly collided with old Mrs Jenkins from number three. She grabbed at my sleeve as I tried to get past her.

'I think you've still got that dog in your flat.' She screwed up her nose in disgust.

I shook myself free of her bony fingers. 'I don't care what you think, you stupid old bat!' I shouted over my shoulder. I raced out after Jago.

I could see them; they were only halfway down the road. As usual people were oohing and ahhing over Tia and she was loving it.

'Trouble?' Jago said, when I caught up with them.

'Not really,' I lied. I wondered if he'd heard me screaming at Linette. Probably. I felt ashamed.

There were plenty of people already out and about, and the sunshine was bright and warm. We reached the harbour car park and wound our way in and out of people and parked cars.

'Carreg is very blue, isn't it,' Jago said.

'What do you mean?'

'The lamp posts, the railings, the benches, even the litter bins, they're all painted the same colour blue.'

I looked around in amazement. He was right. I'd lived here all my life and never noticed that before.

From the top of a CCTV camera a gull with greedy yellow eyes glared down on us.

'Let's go to the Shiver Stone,' I said. We walked the steep incline of St Winifred's Hill and soon left the noise and bustle behind us in the main street.

Tia was already getting tired in the heat, so we stopped halfway up. I took a bottle of water out of my bag, poured some into my hands and watched Tia drink.

We leaned on the metal railings overlooking the harbour. I liked watching the harbour from there. Apart from the passing cars it was quieter and almost like a painting with the brightly coloured boats and buoys bobbing in the water.

'You see that boat there, the red one with the blue stripe?'

Jago nodded.

'That's Dad's boat – *Sea Spirit*. He loves that boat.'

'Your dad's a fisherman,' Jago said. 'What does he catch? I mean, what sort of fish?'

'Whelks,' I said.

'I don't think I even know what a whelk looks like.'

'Think big snail with a grubby shell,' I said. 'People say they're delicious boiled with a drop of vinegar.' I made a puking action with my finger in my mouth.

'Not a fan, then?' Jago laughed.

A sudden shadow made us turn around. A huge figure towered over us. Hug Howells, dressed in her big man trousers and a floppy black t-shirt, did an odd little wave.

Her voice boomed out. 'Um, sorry about yesterday, kids.'

Tia jumped up at her tree trunk leg and, without thinking, Hug bent down to pat the little dog's head lovingly.

'I was just er … having a bad day, I suppose.' Her heavy moon face went red and her eyes shifted away from us. 'Yes, that's it. Bad day. No harm done, huh?'

Jago shook his head. I said, 'No.'

'Right. Good. Good. No harm done.' She took a sudden interest in Jago. 'And you must be Tristan's boy? Yes. I can see that you are. Although he has the look of a blond American Indian with those plaits of his.'

For a minute I thought she was going to pat Jago's head like she'd patted Tia's but, with a repeat of, 'Well. Good. No harm done,' she went on her way down the hill towards the shops.

'Crazy,' I said.

We reached the start of the cliff path. Gulls screamed and flew somersaults over our heads. From this height we could see the bay spread below us. The further along we went the fewer people we saw and that suited me fine. Jago and Tia were quiet company and that's just what I needed.

There's a small woodland near the path and a river bubbles down to Glen Beach. This is my favourite part of Carreg. Even in summer it's peaceful and the birdsong is strong and clear. Here, with the sun bright and warm and the familiar rush of the sea below, I feel happy.

When we reached the giant Shiver Stone, we saw a figure sitting beside it at the edge of the cliff.

She was staring out at the bay. If I hadn't recognised the binoculars and the short black hair I would certainly have recognised the thick snake-like scar running down her back.

She seemed so lost in thought I was afraid, if I spoke, it might startle her and she'd fall.

Jago obviously hadn't thought of that.

'Hello,' he called.

She jumped, but grabbed at the grass on either side of her to steady herself. She scuttled back from the edge and got up to face me. She looked strange, blank.

'This is the Shiver Stone?'

'Yes.'

'It's magnificent.' She brushed her hand over the surface of the rock with affection.

Jago handed me Tia's lead and took a few nervous steps towards the edge. He peered over. 'Wow, you said your dad dived off here when he was a kid? Awesome.'

The woman who'd rescued Jago was now looking at Tia with the same blank stare. 'And this little creature belongs to Tristan. He must love her very much. We all love our pets, don't we? They are special in our lives.'

It was a weird thing to say, and she didn't sound like she meant it. She sounded almost angry.

A cloud covered the sun and the shadow of the Shiver Stone grew longer and darker. Jago was still peering down over the cliff at the sea below. I picked Tia up and cuddled her into me. I thought for a minute. 'How's the birdwatching going? Have you seen the lesser-spotted seadrake?' I asked. 'They're very common around here.'

'What? Oh yes, loads of them.' She seemed nervous, awkward. She was rubbing at the back of her head and it made her hair stick up. 'I've got to go,' she said and hurried away back in the direction of town.

We watched her for a short while and then Jago shrugged.

He took his little hammer thing out of his geology bag and, before I realised what he was going to do, started chipping at the Shiver Stone.

'Stop it!' I said.

He ignored me. 'Just want a piece for my collection. It's a type of rock called spotted dolerite, an igneous rock like basalt. It comes from the Preselis near Fishguard.'

'Stop it. When a tourist tried to chip off a bit of

the Shiver Stone he found all his tires were flat when he got back to the car park. He had to call out the RAC,' I said.

'I haven't got a car,' Jago murmured. Chip, chip, chip.

'When a local kid spat on it, he fell off his bike and broke his ankle a week later.' I was getting angry.

'Don't spit and haven't got a bike,' Jago said. Chip, chip, chip.

'STOP!' Without thinking, I punched his arm. The hammer flew out of his hand and crashed into a nearby bush. 'Don't hurt it!' I screamed, close to tears.

Jago stared at me in amazement. 'If it means that much to you, you should have said,' he muttered.

While he rummaged through the leaves looking for his hammer, I closed my eyes, put both hands on the Shiver Stone, and whispered that I was sorry.

Jago sulked for a while, but I pretended to be interested in his geology stuff and he soon came around.

Tia was getting hot and tired again, so I carried her as we headed back home.

'Funny we keep bumping into that woman,' Jago said.

'Hmm. I'll tell you something funny. She's no birdwatcher.'

'How do you know?'

'Those lesser-spotted seadrakes she said she'd seen?'

'Yeah.'

'No such bird. I made it up.'

I was hoping Dad would be in bed by the time we got back; he'd been fishing all night, so he should be tired. He was fast asleep – the flat quiet except for his snoring. I made sandwiches for us, and chopped up the rest of the tinned ham for Tia.

I'd done some thinking on our way back home and, as we tucked into our cheese and pickle, I said, 'What if your dad has been kidnapped?'

Jago almost choked. 'Kidnapped? Why would you think he's been kidnapped? You saw him run off.'

'Yeah, but there's a lot of odd stuff going on. Maybe there's a secret society after him. Remember the tattoo? Your dad has the same tattoo as that Kemble Sykes.'

I jumped up. '*Vulpes Vulpes* – we can Google it. I'm not allowed to use my laptop but you can.' I was excited. 'We should have done this before. That tattoo could be a clue.'

'A clue to what?'

'I don't know, just a clue.'

Jago typed '*Vulpes Vulpes*'.

'It means Red Fox.'

'What else?'

He scrolled up and down, opened more sites. 'That's it, Red Fox.'

'Try some more.'

Jago tapped the computer screen. There were 1,430,000 results for '*Vulpes Vulpes*'.

'We can't search through all those,' he said

It was disappointing. 'Ask your mum about the tattoo, then. She should know.'

'Yes. She's coming out of hospital today, so we'll move into the caravan.'

I could still hear my dad snoring in the bedroom, so when the phone rang, I ran to pick it up before it woke him. I almost tripped over Tia. By the time I'd got my balance back, the phone had stopped ringing. I could hear Dad talking. He came out of his room looking like he was still half asleep. He had his old blue dressing gown over his pyjamas and his hair was sticking up.

I looked at him to see if he was smiling, hoping everything was okay with us again. He wasn't smiling.

'You're on a real roll, aren't you, Carys? That was Jim from the housing association. Mrs Jenkins has been on the phone to them, complaining that we have a dog in the flat. She also says she wouldn't have said anything except that you were very rude when she spoke to you on the steps this morning. So, thanks to you, the dog has to stay outside in the shed.' He stroked Tia's head and she licked his hand. 'Until your dad gets back that is,' he added quickly to Jago. 'You'd better put her in the shed right now.'

'But what about tonight? She can't stay out there all night. She'll be cold and frightened,' I wailed.

'Maybe you should have thought of that before you were rude to old Mrs Jenkins. Maybe you should think before you're rude to anyone. Linette got it right this morning, Carys, you can be a spoiled brat.' He stormed back into his bedroom slamming the door behind him.

I wanted to cry. Dad was furious with me and Tia was banned to the shed. It was a bad day.

It was about to get worse.

'Spose we'd better put her in the shed then,' Jago said.

'We could take her out for another walk? We can't just leave her in there on her own all day.'

'What about if we take her back to my dad's place? At least she'll be in her own home and, when he gets back, she'll be there waiting for him.'

'But then she'll be too far away and still all on her own.'

I picked Tia up and rubbed my face in hers. She squeaked and wagged her tail and that made me feel even worse.

I got two bowls and filled them with cornflakes and milk. That would do for dessert. 'Besides, what if your dad doesn't come back?'

'What do you mean?'

'Well, if he has been kidnapped...'

I ignored the look of horror on Jago's face and went on.

'I mean he can't just be hiding away from that man, can he?'

Jago walked away from me and went out onto

the balcony and I followed him, carrying the bowls of cornflakes.

'He must know your mum nearly died; that she's in hospital.'

'How would he know?'

'If he's hiding in the village, someone would tell him. Everyone knows everything in Carreg. And unless he's committed a terrible crime or…'

'Shut up! Shut up!'

Tia leapt at Jago's leg, barking. He ignored her.

'How would you like it if someone said your dad was some murdering maniac? What your dad said was right, you are a brat.'

'I'm sorry, I…'

Jago slammed out of the flat.

Brilliant. Now everyone hates me, I thought. I placed both bowls of cornflakes down on the floor for Tia to lap up the milk. And then sat at the table with my chin in my hands, watching the sea mist roll in and cover the Shiver Stone.

CHAPTER

10

I wasn't exactly flavour of the month: Dad was still mad, Linette hardly speaking and now even Jago was ignoring me. We were in a group outside Polly's caravan, sitting on an odd mix of chairs and stools owned by the park. Polly wanted to thank us, so we'd come for a meal of lettuce leaves and fruit. No wonder she was so skinny.

Don't know why Dad was still angry. I'd apologised to Linette – sort of.

The caravan park was crowded; small kids ran

around screaming, music played from several different places at once. Everywhere, wet clothes and towels flapped like flags in the breeze. The smell of barbeques cooking made me hungry.

Dad was deep in conversation with Polly. She was telling him about her Kirlian photography but Dad wasn't buying it. He kept shaking his head and rolling his eyes. They were laughing though. Linette and Jago were talking about, of all things, geology. Yeah, rocks and stuff.

'You can find jellyfish fossils in Carmarthenshire,' she told him. Jago got really excited about that. He'd plaited his hair. He was trying to copy his dad because Hug Howells said Tristan looked like an American Indian. I thought it just looked dumb.

Tia was my only friend. She lay curled on my lap, her fur hot and prickly on my bare legs.

So, when Linette realised she'd left the Welsh cakes on the table in our flat, I volunteered to get them. I thought they'd say no, but they didn't. Dad just handed me the door keys.

I clipped on Tia's lead and strolled down past the Coppet Hall Visitor Centre and across the beach. I didn't think anyone would make a fuss about a dog being there at this time in the evening, especially such a very small dog. I walked slowly picking up bits of shell and odd shaped pebbles. No point hurrying. No one was going to miss me. I sat on the sand throwing stones for Tia to chase.

By the time I got home, collected the Welsh cakes and headed back, the tide was lapping at the shoreline. Unless Tia and me wanted to get very wet I'd have to brave the Troll Hole to get to the caravan park.

I felt a nervous flutter in my stomach, but then remembered how I'd run through it when I was looking for Tia. Not worried at all then. It was time for me to stop being so stupid – I wasn't a little kid anymore.

It was the longest Troll Hole. The one I hate the most. Still it was early evening and there should be loads of people wandering through. I had Tia with me as well.

I gazed into its depths: the darkness, the creepy leaking water-drip; a wind as cold as stone blew through.

A family came hurtling out of the gloom, the kids running ahead half afraid half excited. I bent down and pretended to tie my shoelace. I needed time to calm my heartbeat and get my breathing under control. Tia tugged at the lead and looked up at me with a puzzled frown on her face.

I took a long shuddering breath and dived in.

I made myself walk slowly, every bit of my brain screaming run, run, run. I didn't. I wouldn't. There was a horrible under-stone damp smell, and my footsteps echoed. I realised, with a stab of fear, that there was no one else inside the tunnel with me. It was just Tia and me alone in the dark.

Trolls, my brain whispered. Invisible. 'Stop it!' I said out loud. I kept up a strong steady march. I couldn't see Tia on the lead in front of me. I couldn't see anything. Teeth, claws, my brain murmured. A drip of icy water landed on my head and I shuddered. Then I heard the other footsteps. Good I thought – someone else in the Troll Hole. I'm not on my own. I slowed down waiting for them to catch up. We'd laugh, say how creepy it was in the tunnel, and I'd walk with them to the end. I tucked the bag of Welsh cakes up under my arm. The footsteps slowed down too. I stopped to listen. The footsteps stopped too. I could hear my own breathing loud in my ears. I turned back and thought I could make out a darker shape – the shape of a man. My heart was beating so hard it hurt. With a cry somewhere between a shout and a scream, I ran.

The footsteps ran after me and they were getting closer. Tia thought it was a game and jumped up at me. For a horrible second her lead caught in my legs and I thought I would fall. I stumbled, steadied myself against the wet walls, and raced on. The footsteps grew closer. At last I saw the arch of light and almost sobbed with relief. Just as I reached the end, a hand grabbed my arm. 'Kid, kid, wait!' It was Kemble Sykes.

'Let go!' I screamed.

A large group of teenagers arrived. Shouting and laughing, they got off their bikes and I scuttled through the middle of the chaos, almost dragging Tia off her feet.

Kemble called after me. 'Kid, I didn't mean to scare you! If you know where Tristan is, tell him … tell him: I'm here to warn him. Tell him, it's not me he should be afraid of … it's her.'

I ran as fast as I could back to the caravan park, Tia leaping and jumping beside me, thinking this was great fun. I reached Dad and the others shaking and breathless and blurted, 'In the tunnel, he grabbed me … wants Tristan…'

Dad was on his feet before I had a chance to finish and he raced off towards the Troll Hole. If I thought Dad was angry earlier, it was nothing to the murderous look he had on his face now.

Linette put her arm around me. Jago looked worried and not sure what to do. Polly insisted I have a couple of drops of something called Rescue Remedy on my tongue to calm me. It was a while before I realised the Welsh cakes were now a bag of crumbs.

Dad came back, panting and talking on his mobile. I think it was probably lucky for Kemble Sykes that he hadn't hung around. 'Thanks, Sian, I'll drop by with her tomorrow. It's becoming an odd business. There's some character hanging around the kids. I don't like it. Bye.' He slipped his phone back in his pocket.

'That was Sian at the police station,' Dad told us. 'She called me earlier, said you two had been in to tell them Tristan was missing?' Jago and I nodded. 'I thought you were just wasting her time and I said so. Now I'm not so sure. You reckon this guy in the tunnel is after Tristan – do you know him?'

'His name is Kemble Sykes,' I said.

The effect on Polly was immediate and startling.

'Kemble Sykes? My God I thought I'd seen and heard the last of him.' She sank back down into her chair. Grabbing her wine glass, she filled it and took a big swallow.

Jago was the first to speak. 'Who is he? Why is he after my dad?'

We were all watching her waiting for an answer.

'OK. I owe it to you all to tell you what I know, although it's not much.'

The caravan park was much quieter; as the sun went down, lights appeared in scores of windows all over the camp as kids were put to bed. Crickets chirped in the hedges and people spoke in whispers.

Polly dabbed at the line of stitches on her forehead, took another big sip of wine and turned to face her son.

'Years ago, when we were in Swansea University together, there was a group of us who were against fox hunting. It was legal then. It was a vile, cruel sport. Killing foxes, taking pleasure in seeing them hunted down and ripped apart by dogs. There was about eight or nine of us at first. Kemble was the leader. I suppose you could say Tristan was his right-hand man, but really Tristan just did whatever Kemble told him to. We joined the Hunt Saboteurs Association.

'We'd go out on hunts and do whatever we could to save the fox from being killed. Shouting and blowing horns at the dogs to distract them. Spraying the ground with aniseed or citronella, strong smells that covered the scent of the fox. It was good at first – fun even. We were thrilled every time we saved a fox from the hunters.

'But it was too tame for Kemble. He wanted more action, more violent action. He wanted us to start our own group. We called ourselves *Vulpes Vulpes.*'

'Red Fox,' Jago said.

Polly seemed surprised that he knew what it meant. 'Yes. Red Fox. Most of us were content to wear identity bracelets or medallions with the name on but not Kemble. Oh no, Kemble got it…'

'…tattooed on his arm,' I interrupted.

Again Polly looked surprised. 'Yes, so of course Tristan had to do the same.'

She hesitated and took another sip of wine.

Dad topped up her glass and Linette's and placed the bottle beside his chair.

Polly looked from Linette to Dad and then back again.

'I don't know what Tristan is like now, it's been ten years since I've seen him, but then … well then, he was a gentle sort, always the artist. Sweet really, but easily led. And Kemble loved to lead.' Her face flushed with anger.

There was a hiss and clink as Dad levered the cap off a beer bottle.

Polly's voice was soft but strong. The sort of voice you hear reading stories on podcasts and CDs. Bit by bit we shuffled our chairs nearer until we were in a circle around her. Tia settled on my lap and fell asleep.

'Kemble's ideas grew crazier, out of control. One by one we drifted away, frightened by his antics and wild behaviour. He thought that the people involved with the hunt should be punished. I tried to tell Tristan that wasn't right – it made no sense. Save animals? Yes. Hurt humans to do it? How can that ever be OK? I tried to get him away from Kemble's influence, but he seemed fascinated.

'That night, the night Tristan came home

covered in blood, I think they'd been to sabotage a hunt. Tristan had already stopped telling me what they were up to. He knew I didn't approve of Kemble and his schemes. He was frightened, very frightened. All he would say was that something terrible had happened and he had to get away for a while. I begged him to tell me what, but he said for my sake, and your sake, Jago, it was better I didn't know. He told me he'd contact us as soon as things settled down.'

She shrugged and took another long sip of wine. 'And that, folks, was the last time I saw him until a week ago, when he appeared on the news as the man behind the mysterious sculptures of Carreg.' She lowered her voice. 'If Kemble Sykes is here, you can bet he's here to get Tristan. But I don't know why.'

We left not long after that. Everyone seemed a bit down, everyone except me. I was just glad that they were speaking to me again.

As we left, Polly gave Linette a hug. 'I bet you have a lovely aura. I don't have my camera with me, but maybe another time, I can take a picture for you? A small thank you present.'

Linette smiled. 'I'd like that,' she said.

The four of us, me, Dad, Linette and Tia, walked home together through the Troll Hole. Linette kept her arm over my shoulder and part of me wanted to tell her to leave off, but part of me felt all right about it.

When we reached our road Dad said, 'Let's get some fish and chips, I'm starving.'

We sat on a bench, overlooking the harbour, facing St Winifred's Hotel nestled on the high shelf of rock above.

'You just want to sit here so you can look at your darling boat,' Linette laughed.

The *Sea Spirit* clicked and clanged alongside the other boats as they were jostled by the tide.

'Guilty,' Dad said.

I was enjoying my fish and chips and daydreaming again when I heard Dad say, 'It's ridiculous. She's a nice enough woman but she's filled the kid's head with rubbish. Photographing auras indeed.'

'I don't know, Dai. There're all sorts of things we don't understand in this world.'

'You're just saying that because she told you you probably have a lovely aura,' Dad laughed.

Linette laughed too. 'Everything about me is lovely, Dai Thomas, and don't you forget it.'

She turned to me. 'What do you think about all this aura stuff, Carys?'

'Dunno,' I said, because I didn't. I didn't know what to think.

CHAPTER

11

'Please Dad, please,' I begged.

'She can't sleep in the flat, Carys, and that's final. The shed it is.'

'She'll be cold and frightened. It's dark outside.'

'It's the middle of summer and we've put warm blankets in the box. She'll be fine.'

'But, Dad!' I wailed.

'That's enough, Carys. This is your fault, remember. If you carry on like this I'll call the RSPCA or pay for her to go into a kennels.'

That shut me up. 'Okay, okay,' I said.

I found an old stuffed teddy and put it in the box with Tia. I shut the shed door. As I turned I heard her muffled whimpers from inside.

'I'll see you in the morning, little one,' I whispered though the door. She whimpered again. 'Night, girl.' I dragged myself up the steps to our flat feeling sick and miserable.

I couldn't sleep. If Jago was still here I could have talked to him but he was in the caravan with his mum.

Dad wasn't fishing, but Linette was sleeping over anyway. I couldn't stop worrying about Tia locked in the shed on her own. I think I knew what I was going to do even before I went to bed. As soon as I heard them switch off the TV and go to their room, I got up.

I wrapped the duvet tightly around me and shuffled across the lounge floor. I could hear Dad snoring. I found the spare keys in the fruit dish where Dad keeps them. I didn't have hold of them properly and they dropped with a clang. I froze, then counted to twenty under my breath. Dad was still snoring.

The steps were cold on my feet and I wished I had thought to put my flip-flops on. Outside, the street was eerily quiet as I padded down the path. Tia heard me coming. Her joyful little bark echoed in the shed. I unlocked it quickly and scooted inside.

She went crazy – leaping into my arms and licking my face with her tiny tongue, all the time whimpering with joy.

I laughed out loud. 'You didn't think I'd leave you here alone all night, did you, girl?'

I stacked some of Dad's birdhouses against the wall, brushed a bunch of wood shavings out of the way and arranged the duvet on the floor. Tia snuggled in beside me, gave a little sigh of happiness and immediately fell asleep. I cuddled her tight. She smelled like sunshine and sea salt.

I don't know how long we'd been sleeping when Tia's sudden bark woke me. The beam of a torch light flashed across the window and lit up the inside of the shed. Frightened, I held my breath and watched as the door handle turned very slowly, one way and then the other. Tia was barking like a mad thing and leaping up at the door.

'Who's there?' I shouted. I hadn't planned to shout and I surprised myself. I surprised the person trying to break in too – they dropped the handle with a clank. I could hear footsteps on the gravel.

I quickly switched on the light, opened the door and peered right and left into the darkness. I couldn't see a thing. Even after locking the shed I was too scared to go back to sleep. I pulled the duvet over my eyes and cuddled up to Tia until the light of dawn came in through the window.

Sleepily, I dragged myself back up to the flat. Tia would be okay now it was daylight and I needed some real sleep. I had to get back in my bedroom before Dad woke. He'd go crazy if he knew I'd slept in the shed all night. I couldn't even tell him that someone had tried to break in. To steal, what? His birdhouses?

Luckily for me he was still snoring.

I noticed bits of wood shavings and sawdust stuck to my duvet. They left a trail behind me across the lounge floor and down the hall. I fell onto the bed, and into a deep sleep. Just before dropping off I had a thought: Kemble Sykes had shouted, 'It's not me he should be afraid of, it's her.'

What if the her was Polly? We only had her word for what happened. What if she was lying and Tristan was hiding from Jago's mum? What if she wanted to hurt him in some way? The first birds were beginning their early morning chirping as I closed my eyes. But that was a good story Polly told, too good to be a lie, I thought. So who was the mysterious woman Kemble wanted to warn Tristan about? My eyes were sore and my eyelids heavy. Just before I drifted off to sleep, I thought I heard my door open softly and then click shut again.

The doorbell ringing woke me. It was Jago.

When I came out of my room he was sitting with Dad and Linette on the balcony. I could smell bacon and eggs.

'You look rough. Bad night?' Dad said.

'Mmm.' I hurriedly checked the floor but there were no telltale signs of the shavings and sawdust I'd dragged into the flat the night before.

'Fancy a cooked breakfast?' Linette got up and went into the kitchen. She came back with a huge plateful of food.

'I don't like beans,' I said.

She sighed, went into the kitchen and I heard her scraping the baked beans into the bin.

'Okay now, madam?'

'Okay now.'

Dad gave me a dirty look.

'Thank you,' I mumbled.

Jago and I hurried downstairs and collected Tia from the shed. She jumped up and down in happy excitement.

'I think we should approach this like detectives,' Jago said. 'I've brought my geology notebook and we can make notes and jot down clues.'

I thought this sounded a bit geeky but I had nothing better to do. Then Jago said something really sad. 'I wish I had a dad like yours. In fact I wish I had a dad.'

I knew how he felt. I was sick of being asked, 'Where's your mum?' Tired of trying to explain. Tired of pretending it was okay, that it didn't bother me that my mum loved a load of other kids more than she loved me.

'Right,' I said, 'let's find this missing father of yours, shall we?'

We sat on a bench in the sensory garden. It's where my friend Becca and I go when we want to talk in private. Each bench is surrounded by a high thick hedge, so it feels secret. Tia lay on the warm concrete between our feet.

Jago spoke aloud and wrote neatly in his notebook. 'Ten years ago, Tristan, covered in blood and terrified, leaves Bristol. Abandons girlfriend and two-year-old son.' He went over what he'd written and underlined abandons. 'Ten years later, turns up in Carreg.'

'He didn't just turn up ten years later though, did he?' I corrected him. 'He's been living here for ten years.'

Jago grunted and crossed out turns up. 'Tristan sees frightening character from past and runs away.' His pen seemed to be running out of ink and he shook it several times. 'Question one – what terrible thing happened in the past to make him so scared?'

He stared at me. I said, 'Don't look at me like that – I don't know.'

'Question two, where is he hiding?'

'We don't know that either, do we.'

This wasn't going so well.

'Question three, I can't even think of a question three,' Jago said closing the notebook. 'We're rubbish detectives.'

A head appeared around the hedge. It was Polly. 'Linette said you might be here.'

Linette says too much, I thought. I saw the line of stitches above Polly's eye wasn't quite so swollen, but there was a yellowish bruise near her nose.

We made space on the bench for her to sit down. Jago quickly stashed his notebook away. He didn't want his mother to see it.

'I thought you two could give me a guided tour of Carreg. All I've seen so far is the inside of a hospital room. I'd like to take some close-up shots of the Shiver Stone too. I bet it has an amazing aura,' Polly said.

'I can't, Linette is doing a birthday lunch for Dad today,' I said.

'Oh yes, she asked if we'd like to come, but I think Jago and I have imposed on your family more than enough.'

She turned to Jago. 'I've decided to give it one more day, Jago. If your father doesn't turn up by tomorrow morning we're getting the train back to Bristol.'

'But, Mum…'

'No. I've made up my mind. I feel like a fool

hanging around just in case that man decides to show his face. Whatever happened, whatever he's afraid of, he's got just one more day to prove he's worthy of being your father, Jago. It's his last chance. If we're on that train tomorrow I will never contact him again and that's final.'

She sounded breathless, angry.

Jago and I were silent.

Polly breathed through her nose and fanned her face with her hands. I could see she was trying not to cry.

'Let's go back up to his place. He might be home now. We could try one more time,' Jago said.

'I can't go there. You know that.'

'Why?'

'Bees, Jago, bees! Buzz, buzz, buzz, remember? I don't want to end up back in the hospital. Now how about you take me to the Shiver Stone?'

Jago hoisted his geology bag over his shoulder and got up. As they moved away he turned, flicked his blond plaits over his shoulder and gave me the saddest look.

I sighed. 'Come on, Tia,' I said.

CHAPTER
12

'So where's Dad?'

'Gone to Carmarthen, he's got some business at the bank.' Linette looked guilty for some reason. 'Seeing as it's his birthday, let's call a truce and try to get on for once, Carys, shall we?'

I nodded.

Linette was dressed up for the occasion in a bright pink dress and high heels.

She looked me up and down, taking in my scruffy shorts, t-shirt and flip-flops.

'Maybe you'd like to change into something nice?' she said.

'Maybe I wouldn't,' I answered.

Linette sighed. 'Okaaaay. I've brought some bits and pieces from the Crab Claw and I thought we could make a birthday cake together.' She arranged dips and crisps and party food on plates as she talked.

'Trifle,' I said.

'What?'

'I always make a trifle. I make Dad a birthday trifle every year.'

Linette shrugged. 'That's fine, you can still do a trifle. I'll make the cake.'

She stood behind the kitchen counter and started talking like she was a TV chef. 'Cream together the butter and sugar until light and fluffy, then beat in the eggs.' She did the whole mixture like that. I had to struggle not to laugh.

I put sponges into another bowl, dissolved green jelly with boiling water and poured it over. I carefully placed the bowl in the fridge.

Linette had put the cake in the oven to cook and was washing up. Every now and then she glanced at me. I could tell she wanted to say something, something important, and I didn't want to hear it.

'Carys,' she said at last.

Here we go, I thought. 'I'm just gonna watch telly while the jelly sets.'

'No, wait, I want a word with you. I thought we could have a little talk.'

I sighed. 'What about?'

'It's um … it's been fun this morning, hasn't it? You and me doing stuff together?'

'Yeah…'

'Thing is, me and your dad, well, it's getting serious.'

I felt my mouth go dry. I licked my lips.

'We were wondering how you'd feel about us being a family. You know, the three of us living together.'

'No,' I said.

'No what?'

'No thank you,' I said sarcastically.

'That's not what I meant and you know it.'

I found myself rummaging in the fridge. I didn't want to talk about this. I didn't want to talk about this at all.

I took the bowl of jelly out and shook it. It

was still runny but I added the tin of custard anyway.

'It's going to happen, Carys, you might as well accept it. Your dad and I – well, we love each other. I'm not so bad am I?' She was following me as I wandered around the lounge still carrying the bowl of half-made trifle.

I felt cornered. Angry.

'I'm not trying to take your mum's place, Carys.'

At the mention of Mum the anger went up a notch.

'I'm too young anyway. I could be like your older sister, we could have lots of fun.' I heard the panic in her voice – this wasn't how she thought our 'little talk' would go.

'No,' I said again. 'No!' Louder this time. 'We're okay on our own. I don't want you here.' I could feel the tears coming.

Linette's face went almost as red as her hair.

'Well tough, because me and your dad have already put a deposit on a house together.'

She clapped her hand over her mouth in horror. 'Oh God, I wasn't supposed to tell you that. Dai wanted to tell you himself. He…'

Without thinking I hurled the trifle at her.

Some of it hit the wall but most landed right on target.

I don't know who was more shocked, Linette or me. She stood rigid, as clumps of green jelly, sponge and custard slid slowly down her face and hair, slipped onto to her shoulders and rolled down her new pink dress.

'I … I…' I began.

Linette was quick to retaliate – out of nowhere a dollop of cold cheese dip landed on my head. I inhaled sharply. Grabbing the bowl of peanuts, I chucked them just as Linette ducked down behind the sofa. They pinged off the walls and scattered over the furniture and floor like hailstones.

She came up laughing and rushed to the table. I reached it first and got her in the eye with a fresh cream doughnut. I was laughing too now.

I ducked a ham sandwich. 'Ha, missed!' A pepperoni pizza came hurtling through the air like a frisbee.

Food flew back and forth and we were both laughing so hysterically we didn't hear the key in the front door.

Dad was wearing his best suit.

Linette and I stopped and stood to attention, eyes wide, like naughty school kids.

He walked into the lounge, looked around in astonishment, and said, 'What the hell...'

We looked guiltily at each other.

'We thought we'd throw a party for you,' Linette said, sheepishly.

'Well, you didn't have to throw it all over the house,' Dad said.

And that did it – we collapsed with laughter. Linette fell into the sofa shrieking and holding her stomach. I was laughing so hard I thought my legs would give out, so I dropped onto the floor where I rocked and rocked, unable to stop.

When I managed to control myself, I saw Dad hadn't moved an inch. He looked even more bewildered.

He shook his head. 'I just don't get you two,' he said. He stepped across to where Linette lay gulping for breath on the sofa. He stuck a finger in the green and yellow goop in her hair, put it in his mouth and sucked. 'Nice birthday trifle, Carys,' he said, and that started us off again.

This time Dad joined in. I can't remember the last time I'd heard him laugh like that.

We cleaned up the mess together, scraping food off the wall and the carpet and the window and door. We searched for peanuts, making it into a contest to see who could find the most. Linette won. Then there was a race for the shower – I won. I riffled through Linette's shower gels and shampoos and picked the nicest smelling ones.

When I came out, Linette was waiting outside the door.

'If you don't tell your Dad I spilled the beans about the house we're buying, I won't tell him you slept in the shed with Tia. Deal?' she whispered.

'You know about that?' I whispered back.

'Did the same thing when I was your age, 'cept it was a guinea pig. Deal?' she said again.

She held up her hand for a high five. I slapped it. 'Deal,' I said.

Before she slipped past me into the bathroom, I whispered, 'So if you were like my older sister, would that mean I could use your stuff anytime I wanted?'

'Don't push your luck,' Linette said.

I thought for a minute.

'S'pose we could give it a try,' I said.

Later, we sat down to what was left of the food – a bowl of crisps, two small pasties and some chicken drumsticks.

Linette gave Dad a new jumper that was way too trendy for him, and I gave him a Country and Western CD I knew he wanted.

We did the cake and Happy Birthday singing bit. After Dad had blown out the candles, Linette took the cake back into the kitchen to cut it into slices. And also, it was pretty obvious, to give Dad a chance to talk to me.

He began a spluttering, coughing, red-faced discussion about how we could make a lovely little family and we could all get on if we tried, couldn't we?

I waited until he stuttered his way through the news about the house they were buying. How lovely it was, near the sea still, closer to the Shiver Stone, and with a garden. He told me my room would be much bigger and I could decorate it any way I wanted.

'So, what do you think, Carys, eh?'

'I think I could eat a slice of that birthday cake,' I said.

'No, I mean about the house? About us being a

family. About you, Linette and me living together?'

I waited a second or two, pretending to be thinking it over. Dad swallowed nervously.

When I thought he was just about to explode with nerves, I said, 'All right.'

Dad's eyes nearly popped out of his head. He sat there staring at me.

'Piece of cake?' I said.

Dad knocked over the chair in his hurry to get up.

Linette, who had obviously been listening behind the door, came back in, raised her hand in the air. I high fived it. We grinned.

Dad was hysterically happy, so I decided now would be a good time to ask if I could sneak Tia back in. He only hesitated for a minute.

'Don't let Mrs Jenkins catch you,' he said.

I couldn't get down to the shed fast enough.

I opened the door to be greeted by the forest smell of clean wood and sawdust. I popped my head around the corner, waiting for the squeaks and squeals of pleasure.

There were no squeaks and squeals – there was no noise at all, because there was no Tia.

Her box was empty, her lead still attached to the wall. She couldn't get out. At first I just stood there in disbelief. She couldn't get out. The door was shut tight and anyway I'd tied some string to her lead just in case.

I circled Dad's workbench, tossed aside planks of wood, rummaged through pots of glue. I ran outside, shouting her name, and ran back inside the shed again.

I looked under her box, unfolded the blanket, even shook the stuffed teddy. And all the time I knew – she was gone and not of her own free will. Someone had taken her.

I took the steps back up to the flat two at a time.

'She's gone,' I howled. 'Someone's stolen Tia.'

Dad and Linette hurried out after me. They went through the same process that I'd done: checking under, over, in and out of everything in the shed.

'Stop that wailing, Carys,' Dad said, sharply. 'We'll find her. She can't have gone far.'

'Don't you get it? She hasn't run off, someone's taken her. Tia could be miles away by now. She could be...' I remembered something. 'They tried in the middle of the night. While I was in here, I heard the door. They were going to kidnap her then.'

Too late I realised my mistake.

'You were in here last night? You slept in the shed?' Dad's voice was low with disbelief and his eyes bored into me.

Now I was for it. Dad would ground me for sure and I'd never find Tia.

Linette darted a look at me and then grabbed Dad's mobile out of his pocket. 'I'll call the police,' she said.

'No, wait a minute.' Dad put his hand up to stop her but Linette was already outside the shed and dialing.

'Get the car, Dai. Try in the village, maybe someone has seen her,' she whispered to Dad. She made a shooing motion with her hand. 'Go on, quick.'

He looked confused, but started back upstairs to get his car keys.

I went through the whole crazy search again, even peering under Dad's unfinished birdhouses. Tia was a tiny dog but even she couldn't hide in a shed this small.

Linette's voice was firm on the phone. 'No! She

couldn't have got out by herself. This is serious.'

'Maybe it was my dad taking her back home,' said a voice. Jago was outside, peering in, and looking as panicky as I felt.

'Yes, that's it. That must be it.' I knew it was a daft idea really. Why would Tristan suddenly turn into some nutcase who stole his own dog back? But I needed something to cling onto, so any suggestion that meant she was safe was okay by me. What do they call that? Clutching at straws?

'Let's go and see if he's taken her home,' I said.

I was already running and Jago was close behind me.

CHAPTER 13

Tristan's shed should have looked neglected – it didn't. There was a used coffee cup, on the arm of the sofa, I didn't remember seeing the last time. I found an open packet of biscuits and half a sandwich on the bookcase, too. The stone dust had settled everywhere but you could see footprints on the floor – large and small. But not the prints I was hoping to see – paw prints.

'Someone's been in here recently,' I said. Jago and I had the same thought at the same time and turned quickly to the door. No one. The only sound was a gentle bee buzz in the silence.

'My dad?' Jago said hopefully.

Tristan? I wasn't interested in finding him anymore. I didn't care where he was or who he was hiding from or why. All I cared about was that Tia was missing, maybe hurt, maybe even…

'Do you think Kemble Sykes has got her? Kidnapped her to lure my dad out of hiding?'

This time Jago's idea was a good one, but so frightening I didn't want it to be true.

'Your mum says he's a nutter,' I groaned. I dropped down on to the sofa. 'This is hopeless, she could be anywhere.' I shook myself. I mustn't think like that. I had to find her.

Jago looked as lost and helpless as me. 'What now? If Tia is missing…'

'Tia is missing?' said a voice. Shadowed in the doorway was a man, a tall man, with pale blond hair tied in plaits and wearing a bandana.

'Tristan!'

Jago looked in shock from me to his father and then backed away, as if from a ghost.

'Where have you been? Tia's been stolen!' I

shouted. I was so angry. This was his fault, I was sure of that.

Tristan spoke to me and gave a shy glance at his son. 'Who's taken her? Why? Please, sit down.' This was to Jago, the first words he'd spoken to his son in ten years.

Jago sidled onto the sofa beside me, but kept his eyes firmly fixed on the ground.

'Tell me what happened.'

I did.

'Have you tried the RSPCA? The police?'

'Of course we have.'

As if in a dream, he opened the fridge and took out two cans of fizzy drink. I took one. Jago shook his head. He was still staring at the floor.

'Kemble Sykes might have her.'

At the dreaded name Tristan shot a frightened glance at me. 'You know Kemble?'

'He's been following us around, trying to get to you. Why have you been hiding? Where have you been hiding? Why are you so afraid of him?'

'Whoa, whoa.' He put his hands up to stop me. 'Too many questions at once. Where have I been? That's the easiest one to answer. I've been staying with Hug Howells.'

'Hug? But she…' Suddenly, everything made sense. 'You were there, weren't you, the other morning when Tia was scratching at her door? She recognised your scent and that's why she was crazy to get in. So Hug acted all mean to get rid of us?'

'Yes, she hated doing that, especially turning Tia away. She loves Tia. I knew Tia would be safe with you, Carys. Knew you'd look after her like she was your own. Why have I been hiding? That's an easier question. I was scared. I refuse to be scared anymore.' Tristan paced the floor, his eyes on Jago the whole time. 'I knew Kemble was staying at the Seaview, the guesthouse across the lane. We watched him sneaking around here several times, trying to find me. Hug is a good woman. She knows what happened, what I did, and she still took me in. I couldn't let you know in case you told Kemble.'

Jago hadn't said a word. He shuffled his feet, checked his fingernails, twisted his hair, but not once did he raise his eyes to look at his father.

'I don't care what you did, I just want to find Tia.'

Tristan stopped pacing. 'And you're Jago. I can't believe you're my boy.'

At any other time that would have been funny. The likeness between them was startling.

He reached out a trembling hand and placed it on Jago's head. 'Do you want to know what happened all those years ago, son?'

'Yes,' Jago said.

The metal door of the shed scraped open. 'Then why don't you tell the boy, Tristan?'

Kemble Sykes made his entrance like some evil movie villain. He sauntered to the centre of the shed, his dark clothes and black beard sinister in the bright sunlight streaming through the windows.

'Tell them what happened to that child.'

Tristan's reaction was immediate. He half-crouched with his fists up like a boxer.

'You tell them, Kemble; it was your fault, the fireworks, everything.'

'I hold my hands up to that,' Kemble said, and, as if to prove it, he held both his hands in the air. 'It was to do with fox hunting, which was legal then.'

'We know about that,' I said. 'We know about *Vulpes Vulpes* too.'

Tristan was slowly circling Kemble, jabbing his

fists at the air but going nowhere near his enemy. He didn't look threatening – he looked silly.

'Tell them what you did,' Tristan said.

Kemble was turning in a small circle, keeping eye contact with Tristan. The result was weird. Like the earth orbiting the sun.

Jago and I watched them from the sofa, hardly daring to breathe.

'Tell them, tell them what happened,' Tristan insisted.

'We threw firecrackers under the horses.'

'You did. You threw them.' Tristan was punching the air with more energy, more anger, like he was working himself up to something.

'I threw them.' Kemble's voice had dropped so low it was difficult to hear him.

Although Tristan's fists were now punching the air closer to him, Kemble kept his arms to his side. He continued his small circles, speaking softly like he was remembering.

'I threw the firecrackers. They caused panic, terrible panic. Horses reared, riders fell off. At first it was funny, we watched the chaos from behind the hedge, remember? We were laughing...'

'You were laughing, Kemble.' Tristan pummelled the air. 'You were laughing like a maniac.'

'At all those people in their bright red coats tumbling off into the mud – but then there was the child…'

'The child,' Tristan said. And he lowered his head.

'We didn't see her at first, but we saw her pony, a white pony. He was crazy with fear: eyes rolling, nostrils flaring, rearing and bucking. She tried to hold on, tried to control him, but she was just a small girl, she didn't have the strength. He bolted towards us, towards a high brick wall. We saw them crash straight into that wall. And we saw the horse fall, bleeding, onto the child.'

I heard Tristan sob. 'He was screaming. That poor animal was screaming and writhing and underneath him the girl was still as death. And what did we do? I'll tell you what we did. We ran away. Real heroes, huh?' He dropped his fists and wiped the tears from his eyes with the back of his hand. 'I still hear that pony screaming in my dreams sometimes.'

Jago and I listened.

'And when we got back to my place, we fought,' Kemble said. He looked at Jago. 'Your father wanted us to hand ourselves into the police. To face whatever we had to. He was desperate to know if the kid was hurt. I wanted to keep quiet. No one knew it was us. That's when we fought.'

'Some fight, it was over in minutes.'

'That was just a lucky punch you threw.'

'But it put you through the plate glass door.'

'I've never seen so much blood,' Kemble said, 'and it was all mine.'

'And then you pulled a knife on me.'

'I was bleeding like a stuck pig. The glass cut me everywhere – my arms, my chin.'

The two men batted the sentences back and forth. Jago and I shifted attention from one to the other as they spoke.

'And I pulled a knife,' Kemble said, softly.

'And you told me you were going to the hospital and then you were coming after me. That you'd find me; hunt me down like the huntsmen after the fox. And I ran away again. But not any more, Kemble. What we did was wrong and I'm done running!'

The last sentence was a shout and without

warning Tristan charged, head down like a bull right at Kemble.

I screamed.

Kemble dropped to the floor, but was quickly up again. 'No Tristan, no!'

Tristan clasped him round the middle and tried a sort of judo throw on him. They tussled and wrestled but didn't seem to be getting anywhere. It wasn't much of a fight. They looked ridiculous.

I saw a fight once outside the pub. It was frightening, horrible, fists and blood. Dad pushed me behind him and hurried me away.

This was more like two small kids in a playground.

Now Kemble had hold of one of Tristan's plaits and Tristan was shouting, 'Oh, oh, oh.'

'I said stop!' Kemble shouted. 'I'm not here to hurt you, I'm here to warn you!' They were grunting and panting and sweating.

Jago and I stood up to get a better view.

At last Tristan managed a messy judo throw and Kemble went down, banging his head on the coffee table that Polly had collapsed onto just a few days before.

Kemble sat up, rubbing his head.

'Okay, you win, if that's what you want. Now can I tell you why I'm here?'

Tristan slowly got his breath back and then put his hand out and helped Kemble to his feet.

'Phew! I could do with a cold drink or something. How can you live in this tin can? It's boiling.'

Tristan got another can of fizzy out of the fridge and handed it to Kemble, who sat on the coffee table, still rubbing his head.

'Could I have a drink too … um … Dad?' Jago said, quietly.

Tristan smiled slowly, showing the same gleaming white teeth as his son. He got a drink, handed it to Jago.

'So what's the story?' Tristan perched on the edge of the sofa. His hair had come loose in the fight and he fiddled with it, plaiting it neatly without even looking.

Kemble took a long swallow of his drink. 'It's the girl. Well, she's a woman now. She's out for revenge. She's going to make us pay for what we did. The pony had to be shot and she was seriously injured, could have died.' He was pacing the room restlessly.

'You're crazy.' Tristan frowned.

'No, but I think that poor woman may be.'

His pacing had brought him to the door of Tristan's workroom. He glanced in and said, 'What the hell…?'

'It's a *coblyn*,' Jago and I said together.

Tristan's face flashed with surprise that we knew, but immediately changed back to a frown. 'Never mind that,' he said. 'How did this woman know it was us?'

Kemble dragged his eyes away from the ugly goblin and shrugged. 'Research? It's easy enough on computer. There's stuff on the net about us and how we formed *Vulpes Vulpes*.

'It wouldn't be too difficult to email the others either, ask questions. I know I wasn't Mr Popularity back then. Anyway, trust me, she knows it's us. She probably saw you on telly as well. That's how I knew you were here. Several people made it their business to tell me that someone, with the same tattoo as me, was playing around with mysterious sculptures on a Pembrokeshire Beach. There aren't too many of these around, Tristan.' He held up his arm to show the tattoo.

Tristan began rubbing angrily at his as if he wanted to scrub it away.

While all this talk was going on, I was worrying about Tia.

'Look, I'm going. You don't seem to care too much,' I said to Tristan, 'but Tia is still missing. I've got to find her.'

'Of course I care…'

'Wait. What?' said Kemble. 'That little dog, your dog is missing?'

All three of us nodded.

'Then I may be already too late.'

CHAPTER
14

'My cats, your dog? That's how she's going to do it. God, I suppose, in her mind, they have to pay the price for what happened to her pony,' Kemble said.

This was starting to sound nuts.

'Your cats?' Tristan said, rubbing at his forehead like he was trying to wake up from some dream. Jago and I sat forward, tense and listening, as the day took another weird twist.

'I'll tell you quickly, but we've got to do something if you want to see your dog again.'

The sick feeling crept back into my stomach. Jago grasped my arm.

'She came to work at my clinic.' Kemble stood and began pacing.

'Your clinic?' Tristan said, surprised.

'Yes, I'm a counsellor.'

'A counsellor?'

'Yes, my wife and I...'

'Your wife?'

'For God's sake, Tristan, stop repeating everything I say, you sound like a parrot. Yes, I'm married, with two children and I'm a qualified counsellor with my own clinic. I help people with problems.'

'You do?' Tristan couldn't have sounded more amazed.

'It's not as odd as it seems. After I got myself stitched back together...' Kemble rubbed at his chin. 'This beard hides a six-inch scar, by the way.'

If he expected sympathy he didn't get it.

'While I was getting sorted out at the hospital, I was in a lot of pain and furious with you. A nurse suggested I needed anger management. I laughed then, but a few days later I found myself at a clinic. I learned a lot.

'Anyway, I'm wasting time. In a nutshell, this woman came to work for me. She got friendly with my wife and kids and offered to look after the house and our cats while we went on holiday. When we came back there were no cats and no Emma Carr.'

'Emma Carr – is that her name?' I said.

'Yes.'

Kemble scattered another shower of orange tic tacs into his mouth and chewed. He peered into Tristan's workshop again. 'That really is an ugly thing,' he said.

'It's just something I'm working on,' Tristan said, irritably. 'What happened with Emma Carr? Did you go to the police?'

Kemble took one more nervous look and went on with his story. 'The police weren't interested – suggested she'd accidently lost the cats and then disappeared rather than face the music.'

'Maybe that is what happened.' Tristan had moved so that he was next to Jago on the sofa. I saw him rest his hand lightly on his son's shoulder.

'I would have thought so too, except she left an odd little poem on my desk. She also left a piece of paper with my name and yours. My name had been crossed out with red ink. It gave me the chills, I can tell you. Like some scary movie. I Googled her. That's when I found out she'd had a serious horse riding accident and years of surgery. It happened when she was ten and on a fox hunt near Bristol. It was too much of a coincidence. I knew then I had to get here to warn you.'

A suspicion was creeping into my mind. 'What does she look like?'

'Long fair hair, glasses,' Kemble said.

'There's a woman who's been kind of hanging around us. She says she's a birdwatcher but she's not. She found Tia when we lost her and then when Jago ... um ... fell in the sea...'

Jago gave me a dirty look but didn't say anything.

'When Jago fell in the sea, she helped me pull him out because he can't swim.'

'You could have drowned.' Tristan's grip tightened on Jago's shoulder.

'Yeah. I could have.' Jago gave me another dirty look.

I wanted to change the subject – quickly. 'Can't be her though. This woman's got short black hair.'

'She's got a long scar right down her back.' Jago screwed up his nose.

Kemble turned sharply, waving his hands in the air. 'It's her. It's got to be her. The scar? Back surgery after the accident.'

'But she's got short black hair,' I said again.

'Maybe she's trying to disguise herself. If you've got long blonde hair, you'd change it to short dark hair, wouldn't you? If I could only see a photo or something I'd know if it was her.'

'Anyway, she found Tia when she ran off at the caravan park,' I said shaking my head. 'She was taking her to the police.'

'Are you sure?'

I thought back to when the woman was running in front of me, cradling Tia in her arms. Something wasn't right. Then it hit me.

'You're right,' I said. 'She was trying to hide Tia in her jacket. She hadn't found her, she was taking her.'

'If we could be sure it's the same woman, we could get the police involved,' Kemble said.

'We've got a video of her,' Jago said softly. He turned to me. 'I got bored videoing you diving. I focused in on that woman because she was watching us.'

'We've got to get that video. It's on my phone at home.' I felt hope coming back into my bones – at last we had something, we could do something.

The four of us ran outside.

'I'll drive you,' Kemble said.

'I'd better take Carys on my motorbike. It's faster. Is that okay with you, Jago?' Tristan said.

He nodded.

I snatched the crash helmet from him and leapt astride the bike. Tristan kicked the starter into action.

I held on tight as we bounced along the lane and took a sharp left down towards the village.

With a jolt and a roar we were off down St Winifred's Hill and into the centre of Carreg. The bike smelled of petrol and leather and heat.

The red traffic light held us prisoner. The idling bike seemed to hold its breath. I found myself counting off the seconds.

The green light, another roar, and through the traffic to my street. The first half of our road is all shops and cafes and every tourist in Wales was there that day. We bumped and jerked along as people criss-crossed in front of us, and dawdled along the pavements in hoards. Twice we had to stop to let families with pushchairs pass us. And an old lady on a walking frame took forever to get from one side of the road to the other. It felt like the whole world was trying to slow us down. It was all I could do not to scream.

At our flat, I jumped off and hurtled up the steps.

I thrust the door open. Linette was in her dressing gown, drying her glowing red hair after a shower.

'Where's Dad?'

'Still searching the village for Tia. I said I'd wait here in case the RSPCA called, or the police.'

I was too twitchy to listen. 'My phone?' I said.

'Any news of Tia?'

'My phone,' I said, 'where is it?'

'Carys, you know your phone's been confiscated.'

'You don't understand, pleeeeeease.'

'I can't … Tristan?' The last bit of her sentence was said in shock as the tall figure appeared at the open front door. 'Where have you been?'

'My phoooooooone,' I wailed.

'I'll explain when I can.' Tristan said. 'We really need Carys' phone.'

'But her dad…' Linette was moving towards the sideboard. She opened the drawer, took out my phone and held it to her chest. 'You're going to get me into trouble, Carys. What's so important that you need it now?'

'Jago took a video of me diving. There's a woman on the video we need to check if…'

A sharp knock at the door made me turn. Jago and Kemble stood outside the open doorway.

I beckoned.

Linette was viewing the video on my phone, screwing her eyes up with concentration. 'Oh, nice dive, Carys, I didn't know you could dive like that. Did Dai teach you?'

I stood there, holding out my hand for my phone, getting more annoyed by the second.

Linette rattled on. 'I recognise that woman with the binoculars. She's the reporter I told you about, Carys. The one that came into the Crab's Claw and then followed you down to the harbour.'

'You didn't tell me about any reporter,' I said.

'Really? Must have slipped my mind. She said she wanted to do a follow-up story on the sculptures. She came back and said she'd missed you, so I told her where you live.'

'Good ploy,' Kemble said.

Linette looked up with a start. 'Who the hell are you?'

'He's Kemble. Give him the phone,' I said.

'You're Kemble Sykes? The mysterious skinny-beard guy? But I thought...' She frowned and looked from Tristan to Kemble and back to Tristan.

'He's okay, Linette, honest. Give him the phone.' Tristan said. 'The woman on that video may have Tia. She may be going to hurt her. It'll take too long to explain now.'

Linette reluctantly handed me the phone. I passed it over to Kemble without even looking at it.

His fingers flicked rapidly over the buttons and he studied the screen in silence. We waited.

'It's her,' he said. 'Let's go to the police.'

I turned to go with them, but Linette grabbed my sleeve. 'Wait just a minute.' She said to Tristan, 'Do you really think I'm going to let Carys rush off with you lot when I've got no idea what's going on?'

'Linette.'

'No! Tell me what this is all about.'

'She's right,' Kemble said.

We sat down although I couldn't stop jiggling my legs. I wanted to be off doing something. Who knew what was happening to Tia while all this talking was going on. When Linette asked if anyone wanted coffee, I gave a kind of growl. She deliberately ignored me. 'Or tea?' she said.

Luckily they were as eager to get moving as I was and said no. Kemble told his story honestly, although it didn't make him look good. I noticed Tristan was ashamed – he kept rubbing at his forehead and looking down.

'And she left this little poem,' Kemble was saying. He went into the back pocket of his jeans, took out a wallet and rummaged through. He passed a scrap of paper to Linette. She read it and handed it to Tristan. From Tristan it went to Jago and then to me. I read:

> When all is pain
> And I'm alone,
> My heart and I
> will turn to stone.

Kemble took the paper back from me with a nod and stuffed it back into his wallet. 'I think it's about her pony,' he told Linette. 'He was called White Cloud. He had to be shot after he broke his leg that day.'

As soon as I read that note, I knew. I knew where Emma Carr was. I was never more sure of anything in my life. What I didn't know was whether we would be too late to save Tia.

CHAPTER 15

'The Shiver Stone! That's where she is. Don't you remember, Jago, how fascinated she was by it? And what she said about always going to the Standing Stones when she was frightened or upset? And, when we found her there, she was acting weird. Remember?'

Jago nodded enthusiastically. 'Carys is right. We found her sitting on the edge of the cliff and she was talking about pets and stuff but – not in a good way.'

Linette couldn't stop me this time. No one could have stopped me. I grabbed the crash helmet again.

'Come on!' I shouted at Tristan.

In my panic it seemed like even more people filled the streets of Carreg, that the traffic lights stayed red for longer. But, at last, we burst through and roared up the hill.

Tristan threw the bike against a fence and we jogged on foot through the small woodland, with the river trickle ringing in our ears. We made our way through the trees and bushes. Neither of us spoke.

It was so quiet, so very peaceful, that for a moment I was afraid that I was wrong. That Emma Carr would be nowhere near the Shiver Stone. That maybe we would never find Tia. I forced that thought out of my mind. As we drew closer I could hear the sea booming below.

'Do you think…?' Tristan began.

'Shhh.' I put my finger to my lips.

The sun was setting in a sky of great pink and red streaks that turned the trees to silhouettes.

And there, against the scarlet, stood the massive stone. Beside it, sitting on the cliff edge was Emma Carr. In her arms she cradled Tia.

I drew a sharp breath and barred Tristan with my arm. 'If she sees you...' I whispered. He understood and drew back into the trees.

I moved as silently as I could. I knew I had to get her attention without frightening her. If she dropped Tia...

As I grew closer, I could hear that she was singing a sad song. She was rocking Tia like a baby and, thankfully, Tia seemed to be enjoying it.

Whether I stepped on a twig, or whether Tia smelled my scent, I don't know. But her ears suddenly pricked up and she struggled upright.

Emma tightened her grip on the little dog and turned to face me.

I felt my throat tighten with fear and my heart beat like never before. I smiled. 'I don't believe it,' I said, 'you've found her again.'

It was never going to work and it didn't.

'Get away from me.'

To my horror I saw that she was struggling to stand up, still holding on to Tia. She was so close to the edge that the movement loosened several stones and they rattled over the top and disappeared from view.

'I'm sorry about your pony, Emma.' I kept walking very, very slowly towards her.

She looked startled. 'What do you know about White Cloud?'

'I … I … know he died.'

'How do you know?'

I wasn't sure how to answer her; if I told her Kemble was here it would make things worse.

I tried a different tack. 'You don't want to hurt Tia. She's never harmed anyone. It's not her fault White Cloud died.' I could hear the tremble in my voice.

Emma was still very, very close to the edge of the cliff. Tia was making little whimpering sounds, wriggling to get to me.

Emma began to cry. 'You don't know what it was like. White Cloud was everything to me. They killed him. They terrified him with their fireworks and he bolted. I was in a coma for weeks and, when I came around, my father told me he was dead. That his legs were so badly broken and he was in so much pain they had to shoot him – my beautiful White Cloud.'

She was sobbing hysterically now and I was crying too. But all the time I'd inched closer and closer.

From the corner of my eye I saw Jago, Kemble and Tristan moving like ghosts in the gloom of the trees as they closed in on us.

A lone seagull screeched. The sea crashed its waves onto the rocks far below.

'Please let me take Tia, Emma. Please let me have her.' I held out my arms.

She backed away from me until she was teetering on the very edge. She clutched Tia tightly to her chest.

I leaned my hand against the Shiver Stone, trying to draw courage from its magic. I was distracted for only an instant, but in that instant it happened.

Tia fought for her freedom and she fell.

Life went into slow motion as I saw her tumble from Emma's arms and disappear over the cliff.

The scream that echoed in my head was my own as I ran and leapt and dived off after her.

Down and down and the wind rushed hard and loud and down and down, the world a blur until the hit. An icy shock of dark green sea and the scrape and sting of bottom rocks and up and up again.

I surfaced, gasping, struggling for air. The swell

was strong and the waves lifted me and forced me towards the cliff base. I searched desperately for Tia and, at last, several metres away, I spotted her tiny head, no bigger than a slick, black tennis ball.

Her eyes were wild with fear, the whites shining like marbles. Eight strong strokes and I was beside her. In her terror she tried to climb onto my head and I struggled to hold her.

Swimming with only one arm, grasping Tia with the other, I made for the rocks. The tide was full in and I knew I didn't have the strength to battle the sea for any distance; especially around the headland where the currant made swimming treacherous.

My saturated clothes dragged at my body, but I managed on the third try to haul us out onto the rocks. I collapsed full length, panting with exhaustion. Tia, looking bedraggled and tinier than ever, shivered with shock and cold. I held her close trying to warm her little body with my own. But I had no heat to offer her and we shook, huddled together, as the waves bashed the rocks around us.

My stomach was stinging and lifting my t-shirt I saw the criss-cross streaks of blood. I'd dived so deeply I'd grazed myself on the rocks at the bottom.

I was scared and tired and sore and not sure what to do next. I'd saved Tia from the water but how could I get us back home? We were cut off by the sea and there was no way I could climb back up the full height of steep cliff face to the Shiver Stone.

As I stared up, I saw several people looking down at me. They seemed like shadows in the growing darkness, but the shouts were real enough. They were pointing out to sea and, with a thrill of relief, I saw the bright orange blob of the Tenby inshore lifeboat.

Over the crash and splash of sea I heard the engine throb. It sounded beautiful.

I was worried about Tia – she'd stopped shivering and was limp in my arms. I cuddled her tight, rubbing her tiny body to keep her warm.

'They're coming, Tia. We'll be okay, girl. Don't give up now, please.'

Every second of that wait seemed like forever. But, at last, the boat and the three yellow-clad men were in clear view. I could hear cheers and shouts coming from the cliff top high above me.

They expertly manoeuvered the lifeboat into the gulley between the boulders and, as it bobbed and bucked on the swell of the tide, hauled us aboard.

'Here, my darling,' one man said, 'let's put this around you.' I felt the warmth of the blanket and quickly wrapped Tia in its folds, holding her close and trying to breathe warm air onto her face.

With a clatter the engine roared into life again and we headed away from the cliff.

'Aren't you Dai Thomas's daughter?' one of them said. I nodded, my teeth chattering with cold. It was Becca's Uncle Bryce.

'Tia,' I breathed, 'Tia.' I tried to feel for her heartbeat but my hands were numb with cold.

'She just dived off the Shiver Stone after that little dog,' one of the men said.

There was a gasp of admiration in the boat.

Another shook his head sadly and whispered to his friend, 'All for nothing by the look of it. The dog's in a bad way. '

'No,' I shouted. 'No! Tia, Tia.' I hugged her tiny body in panic and water dribbled from her mouth.

As I held her to me, her eyelids fluttered and a tiny pink tongue came out and licked my nose.

'Well, I'll be...' said the lifeboat man. He turned away, but not before I saw the tears in his eyes.

Tenby harbour grew closer and closer. I saw a group of people had gathered to welcome us in. They were clapping and cheering. Dad burst forward, splashing through the water, and to my total embarrassment, lifted me, still cradling Tia, off the boat.

There was a vet for Tia and a waiting ambulance for me. I kicked up such a fuss when they tried to take her from me that they allowed Tia and the vet to travel to the hospital with Dad and me. It was a short drive, but by the time we got there, Tia had perked up big time.

As soon as I warmed up I was fine. The doctor, and it was Dr Dylan again, made a fuss about the grazes on my stomach, but after he'd treated them, he gave in and let me go home.

Tristan had agreed that Tia should stay with me that night. He'd pick her up the next day.

'To hell with Mrs Jenkins,' Dad said, as he tucked Tia and me up in bed together.

CHAPTER
16

We had a lot of visitors the next day, but when Linette told me who was first in line it was a bit of a shock.

'Emma Carr?' she said. Her eyebrows shot up so high they nearly disappeared into her red hair.

'I think it's a good idea,' Dad said. 'Kemble will be with her. That's if you want to see her, Carys?'

I did. There was something I needed to ask.

When she arrived, Jago, Tia and I were tucking into Dad's beans and cheese on toast.

She came in looking terrified, small and very, very pale.

'I don't know what to say. Sorry isn't anywhere near enough. When I saw you dive off I ... I thought I'd killed you ... and Tia.' She burst into violent sobbing.

Kemble gradually calmed her down but she was in no state to carry on and, after she gave me an awkward hug, they left.

'She's going back to his clinic in Bristol with him,' Dad said. 'She'll get the help she needs. Tristan doesn't want to bring any charges – she pulled Jago out of the sea, after all.'

When Dad went indoors, Jago muttered, 'You pushed me in.'

'Oh, give it a rest, will you.'

After Emma Carr had left, I realised I hadn't asked my question. 'Were you going to throw Tia off that cliff?' Then I thought, maybe she doesn't know herself.

Throughout that day, in bits and pieces, I found out what happened at the Shiver Stone when I did my crazy dive.

Kemble held it together enough to grab Emma

back from the edge. She was hysterical and screaming. He thought it was a real possibility that she would leap off herself.

Tristan and Jago were terrified to look over, expecting to see my mangled body floating on the waves.

'He was crying,' Tristan said, nodding at his son.

'Was not,' Jago said quickly.

It was Dad who called the Tenby lifeboat out – he saw it all. Just after we left the flat, in our frantic rush to get to the Shiver Stone, Dad arrived back from his search for Tia.

'I told him what was happening and he raced off like a crazy man,' Linette said. 'He said he came out of the trees just in time to see you disappear over the cliff. Kemble, Tristan and Jago had a real fight on their hands to stop him diving after you.'

Dad was still very quiet, upset by the whole thing. I tried to cheer him up.

'You're just mad because I've beaten your record by diving off the Shiver Stone when I'm twelve, not thirteen.'

'I thought I'd lost you, Carys,' Dad said. 'I can't laugh about this – not yet anyway.'

But when Linette pointed out that Tia had beaten us both, because she wasn't even two yet, we did get a smile.

'I think he'd like to ground you for a year,' Linette said, 'but I told him having Carys around all day, every day? That's a harsh punishment for us!'

Hug arrived with a whole box full of Hug's Happy Honey. She insisted on apologising all over again.

'You see he…' She gave Tristan a friendly pat on the back, which launched him forward with a jolt and spilt his coffee. '…he may not be the bravest of the bunch but he is a good man.'

I think this was for Jago's benefit.

'He did send flowers while you were in hospital, and got me to ring ten times a day,' she boomed at Polly.

Tristan said, 'I went to visit you too, but chickened out at the last minute. I knew you must already be angry with me.'

'I am,' Polly said.

Another thing I found out was that it wasn't Emma trying to break in to steal Tia from the shed that night. It was Linette, checking to make sure that I was there and that I was all right.

It was two days later and we were squished together on our balcony – me, Dad, Linette, and Jago, Polly, Tristan and Tia. Not a world full of Mrs Jenkinses could make us shut Tia in the shed again. Anyway, when she'd heard the story, and everyone in Carreg had heard at least one version of the story, Mrs Jenkins apologised. She even bought biscuits for Tia. So I told her I was sorry for calling her an old bat.

Tristan looked awkward, shy. 'I'm moving back to Bristol to be nearer Jago. I've got a load of commissions since your video of me was shown on TV so I'll need a bigger studio too.'

He put his arm around Jago. 'I've realised it wasn't just the fear of Kemble that made me run away all those years ago. It was also the fear of being a dad. I used Kemble as an excuse. I was too young, too stupid. I can't believe this amazing young person here is my son. How lucky am I?' They both grinned and looked so weirdly alike that it should have been funny.

Only I wasn't laughing. A cold sick feeling was

creeping into my stomach. If Tristan was moving to Bristol, so was Tia. I would never see her again. My chest tightened and I held her up, pressing her face to mine. She licked my nose.

'There is one big problem though.' Tristan was smiling and looking from Linette to Dad and back again. I thought I saw him wink.

'This apartment I'm moving to. I can't take Tia. And I was just wondering, if now that you're moving into a house, well, I was just wondering if...'

I held my breath.

'...if Carys might like to have Tia?'

I heard a great sob and realised it was me. I turned tearful eyes to Dad, afraid, so afraid, he would say no.

He waited for at least ten seconds before he answered, and every second beat like a drum in my head. It felt like the whole world had stopped to listen to his answer.

Then: 'Don't see why not.'

They all burst out laughing and I realised it had already been arranged. I didn't care. Happiness soared through me like a huge wave and I felt tears trickle down my face. I nuzzled her neck and whispered, 'You're mine, you're mine, you're mine.'

There's just one more thing. I haven't told anyone because they'll think I'm nuts. But I'm not. It happened. I know it happened...

Up on that cliff, seconds before I dived off, when I touched the great stone to give me courage – it shivered.

AUTHOR'S NOTE:

Dear Saundersfoot,

As you've probably realised the town of Carreg is you. I changed a few things – made your tunnels longer, brought the caravan park nearer and gave you the Shiver Stone. This was purely for dramatic effect. In real life you are perfect the way you are. I wouldn't change a single grain of sand.

Sharon Tregenza (author)

ACKNOWLEDGEMENTS

I'd like to thank my publishers the lovely Janet Thomas and the lovely Penny Thomas at the lovely Firefly Press for their help and enthusiasm – they've been a real pleasure to work with. Also, thanks to my friend and fellow writer Judith Barrow for sorting out my comma-phobia. And always and ever I'd like to say a huge thank you to my extraordinary family – The Greigys and The Tregys.

Also from

Firefly Press

Blackfin Sky by Kat Ellis

'A wonderful, compulsive read' Yangsze Choo
'one of my favourite debuts of the year' Luna's Little Library
'An engaging, richly detailed fantasy, full of magic and
mystery' Debbie Moon

Find out more about The Shiver Stone
and our other books at
www.fireflypress.co.uk